THE SHOES OF MOSES

THE SHOES OF MOSES

Stories of ponderable wonder

Blaine C. Readler

Full Arc
Press

THE SHOES OF MOSES

Published by Full Arc Press

Visit us at: http://www.readler.com

E-mail: blaine@readler.com

An acknowledgement and thanks to Lulu Enterprises, Inc. for making the publishing of this book possible. http://www.lulu.com

ISBN: 978-0-9834973-2-5

Printed in the United States of America

First Edition: 2011

This book was previously published as:
"The Worth of Smart," (ISBN: 978-0-615-40038-9)

For Monica, who created the universe that made this work possible.
Now there's a truth you can hang your hat on.

ACKNOWLEDGEMENTS

A very warm thanks to the generous and valuable help in editing these stories, without which they would have included an extra and unintentional level of humor:

Mike Walsh and Renee Fraser

Gail Johnson

Chris and Dan Wilson

Chuck "Chuck" Rothrauff

& (of course) MTB

All you need in this life is ignorance and confidence and then success is sure.
—Mark Twain, Letter to Mrs. Foote

When the truth is found to be lies,
and all the joy within you dies,
don't you want somebody to love?
—Darby Slick

CONTENTS

The Truth About Robots

"You could have told me that your dad was the Robot-man," Shawn whispered.

"He's my dad by sperm only," Taylor replied, "and he probably gave that up with a fight."

He resented his father for many reasons. Cheating his mom was the one he couldn't passively stand by for.

Peering cautiously from the bushes, he saw that the sidewalk along the stuccoed perimeter wall was empty. People who lived in Rancho Santa Fe tended not to walk around at night, not because it was dangerous, but simply because their neighbors would have thought them odd—"Did your chauffeur get drunk and lose his license *again?*"

"Still," Taylor's college friend persisted, "if he were my biological father, I'd have plastered it all over the web."

"If he was your father," Taylor assured, stepping out and grabbing the distinctive baseball cap from his back pocket and pulling it down over his forehead, "you wouldn't be here sneaking in."

"Because we'd have a close relationship, and he would have given me the access code long ago," Shawn played along with feigned heartfelt conviction while slipping a pair of Groucho glasses over his nose.

"No. Because he would have killed you at birth, and nobody would have objected."

Taylor dug out the costume beard from inside his jacket and slipped the hooks over his ears. Holding his hands out in demonstration, he asked, "So, how do I look?"

Shawn eyed him critically. "You look like one of the Three Stooges trying to masquerade as a college professor. The only way you'd be mistaken for the Robot-man would be if the observer were near-sighted and standing a hundred yards away."

Taylor slipped on the nose-clip he used for swimming. "Luckily we won't have to fool a living person."

Now he looked like Moe and sounded like Daffy Duck.

"Your dad's surely going to recognize you when he plays back the surveillance video."

"Probably. But it will be too late by then," he quacked. "My mom will have her ring back, and he would never sic the police on me."

"That doesn't sound like some heartless genius."

"Believe me, he's just watching out for his own ass. He wouldn't think twice about having me thrown in jail. But the last thing he wants is to face my mom in court, so he wouldn't dare give her any excuses."

Taylor started towards the massive entry gate, but Shawn caught his arm. "Wait. Are you saying that your mom doesn't even know that you're doing this?"

He shrugged and shook his head. "How do you think he managed to walk all over her in the first place?"

Now that he was here, standing in front of his father's estate in the plush celebrity suburb of San Diego, he felt suddenly foolish. It was silly enough dressing in a ludicrous fake beard and the quirky Led Zeppelin cap his wealthy deadbeat father was famous for, but he suddenly sagged with doubts about breaking into someone else's house. This was his own father, but a father who was . . . someone else.

The time for second doubts had passed, though; the surveillance camera would have already captured them standing there looking dopey. With one last deep breath, he flipped up the cover on the keypad and punched in the code he'd meticulously memorized, taking care not to touch the fingerprint reader.

"Who be you?" a sensuous contralto voice purred from somewhere above them.

Taylor's mom claimed that the voice was that of his dad's girlfriend, and Taylor didn't doubt it. His father, the Robot-man, took mischievous pleasure in substituting customized versions for all the normal personality selections offered by the appliance manufacturers.

"Why, it's me, David, of course," Taylor replied, trying to make his voice deeper.

"I'm sorry, but you don't really look or sound like David."

The instantaneous response was a little eerie. The woman's voice started talking before he'd even finished his last word. Taylor realized that the surveillance system designers probably added a timed delay to the lightening-fast response of the artificial intelligence, and it would be just like his father to override that for intimidating effect.

"Of course, it's me," Taylor retorted, trying to add the impatient arrogance of the software's true master. "I have a cold."

"Your beard is longer than it was this morning."

"The cold makes it grow faster."

This time there was a noticeable pause. "I'm sorry, but I find no reference of accelerated hair growth as a consequence of viral infections."

He glanced at his friend, but the Groucho disguise made Shawn's expression difficult to interpret. "Google doesn't know everything. I have a unique genetic tendency for this. Now let me in."

"I'm sorry, but I didn't get a fingerprint reading. Could you please re-confirm?"

"It won't work."

"Please wait . . . the reader tells me it's functional."

"No, I mean my fingerprint won't register because . . . my fingers are covered with dry snot. The cold, remember?"

"If you are David, please forgive me, but this is an unusual situation."

Taylor had a hunch that swelled instantly to panic. "Don't call my phone—that's an order."

"You told me that this is the most reliable method to confirm your identity."

This was off-script, and Taylor had to think fast. "This man next to me will kill me if my phone rings."

"Should I call the police?" came the instantaneous and still pleasant voice.

"Negative! He'll know, and he'll shoot me. The only way to save my life is to let us in."

Taylor looked knowingly at his friend.

"I'm going to shoot in three seconds," Shawn growled from under the big plastic nose. "Three—two—"

A green LED and a click announced their admittance, and the gate slid silently out of the way.

"You have six messages," the woman's voice informed brightly, following them along the long driveway via hidden speakers. "Shall I tell the bathroom to prepare the Jacuzzi?"

"Uh, no. I won't be staying long."

"Excuse me, David, but I've concluded that I need to confirm that you do not want me to call the police. This seems important."

"If you call the police, I'll deactivate you—I'll pull out all your memory cube thingies."

"I don't think I understand. Are you telling me that you do want me to call the police?"

"No! Jesus. Do not call the police."

Shawn leaned his Groucho face in to whisper into Taylor's ear. "Kind of dumb, considering she belongs to the Robot-man."

"It's a standard surveillance system," Taylor explained in a normal volume. "My dad—er, I specialize in mechanical aspects."

"I thought he—you—was a genius with nanotechnology."

"Same thing. 'I' somehow make a matrix of the stuff so that millions of these little do-dads all moving together works like a muscle. Something like that, anyway."

"Gee," his friend gibed, "that sounds awfully vague for a genius on the subject."

Inside the black plastic fake rims, Shawn's eyes went wide as he must have realized that he may have given something away.

Taylor smiled. "Don't worry. The system's not that smart. Watch—"

In a louder voice, he said, "Surveillance—who am I?"

"You are David Armstrong."

He took off the nose clip and held it up for her to see. "I repeat: who am I?"

"You are David Armstrong."

To Shawn, he explained, "You see? Once she recognizes me as . . . him, it takes a good bit to convince her otherwise. It's called cognitive hysteresis."

"Are you trying to sound like the genius she thinks you are?"

"No, it's true. Despite myself, I pick things up from . . . him."

They climbed a half-dozen wide steps to a covered landing and stood before massive double doors. Taylor tried the doorknob, but it was locked. "Open, please," he called out.

"Sorry, but I need to confirm that you want to let your companion into the house."

"Of course. Open up."

"Sorry, but I need to remind you that he is possibly dangerous."

"He's changed. He's now my friend. Now open up."

Taylor tried the door, and it swung easily.

As they walked in, the female surveillance chirped, "Welcome David's friend."

The front door opened into a foyer that was just an extension of a cathedral-like living area made all the more massive by the deactivation of central lighting. In the owner's absence, only cubbyholes and corners remained lit, leaving the exact boundaries of the massive space undefined. As soon as they entered, though, brilliant light flooded the indoor canyon.

"Lights off!" Taylor called.

All but one bright overhead spot went dark, and a young boy's voice emanated from that point. "You want the main banks to remain off, David?"

"Affirmative."

"Does that mean you want me to turn them on?"

"No. I was simply agreeing—just leave them off."

The overhead spot winked out, leaving the dimly lit cathedral again enigmatic with indistinct dimensions.

"Do you want me to change the normal entry routine?" the young boy's voice asked.

"No. Just this one time."

"Does this change the lighting procedures now—this one time—for the rest of the house?"

"Correct."

"Is that like affirmative?"

"Yes," Taylor replied impatiently. "Tonight—this one time only—there is no lighting 'procedure.' Got it?"

"I understand. But now I don't know what to do—this one time only."

"Just do what I tell you, and only what I tell you."

"For how long?"

"Shut up, already!"

Instantly every last light was extinguished, and Taylor found himself standing in utter darkness.

From nearby in the blackness, Shawn whispered, "Is he mad at you?"

Taylor sighed. "A-I software doesn't get mad. I think he just tried to follow what he thought was a command." Into the vastness, Taylor called, "Turn the lights back on . . . but just the ones that were on before we came in."

The cubbyholes and crannies glowed forth.

"His voice sounds like you, you know," Shawn observed.

"You're nuts."

"No, it does. I'll bet that's just how you sounded when you were, like, ten."

"Nah. It's probably one of his friend's kids. The refrigerator is Dustin Hoffman." Into the air he called again, "Surveillance, what time did I say I would return home?"

"You said you would probably return between eleven o'clock and midnight," the woman's voice purred. "You have returned early," she added with confidence and apparent satisfaction.

Despite the vacuous depth of intelligence Taylor found the female voice sensuous, almost seductively inviting.

And, considering that the voice was possibly that of a rumored future stepmother, he cringed at his involuntary reaction.

"Okay," he said softly to Shawn, glancing at his watch. "We have a good hour."

"You believe her?" his friend challenged. He moved his head close to Taylor's ear and whispered softly, "What if she knows what we're up to, and she's just trying to trap us?"

Taylor wagged his head. "She can't lie. None of them can."

He'd learned this the hard way. He visited his father only occasionally, and the last time, a week ago, he'd taken the opportunity to snoop into the celebrated man's info-base after he'd fallen asleep, cradled in the numbing haze of expensive Scotch. This was when Taylor had gotten the house access code. The info system had gone idle, and Taylor had gently placed the touch-pad against his father's thumb to log back in.

He hadn't planned this ahead of time, but the opportunity was just too tempting to resist. He knew that the surveillance gal had seen him, and, familiar with her limited intelligence, he'd told her that he and his father were participating in a uniquely human activity, and that his father would be very angry with her if he found out that she'd watched. In fact, Taylor emphasized, his father would likely de-activate her forever if he knew.

An hour later Taylor was watching a movie, and his father suddenly woke with a shudder and sputtered, still half asleep and woozy, "Waa-what's going on?" Taylor knew that this was just involuntary prattle from an addled mind, but she didn't. Dutifully and apologetically, she spilled the beans. In detail. She then suggested that she was a relatively expensive possession and that he might want to consider whether de-activation was wise.

Taylor danced some fancy steps on that one. Casually, and with a pounding heart, he explained that he'd thought he needed to access the info-system to get to the movie library. Sober and fully awake, his father would have caught the lie. But the Robot-man was neither, and he mumbled some observation about the apparent fallacy of inherited intelligence before slipping back into a sloppy slumber.

"So, where are the robots?" Shawn asked quietly as his eye caught with interest a pile of Playboy magazines lying on a table.

"They don't walk around the house pulling chairs out for you. They're not obvious until you use them."

The idea of walking-talking robots had been invented early in the previous century when the most valuable labor-saving device was a servant. An Asimov-style man-robot was the logical imagined automation of that world. The super-wealthy of Taylor's day still retained these servants, but this was purely for show.

"That lamp over there is one of my father's designs."

"A robot *lamp*?"

"Sure. Watch."

Taylor picked up one of the Playboy magazines and sat in the chair beneath the stylishly sculpted pole.

"Would you like illumination, David?" the lamp asked with the slightest lisp, having been informed by surveillance that, although the lamp might think otherwise, this person with the wildly sprouting beard was indeed Master.

"Please," Taylor replied, and the cupped crown arced over and down. Reticulated petals opened, and soft light bloomed on the naked woman in his lap, brightening until Taylor said, "That's fine."

"Huh. Pretty cool," Shawn affirmed. "A robot that could make popcorn, bring me a beer, and then massage my feet would be perfect, but this is still pretty cool."

"This lamp alone costs a year of your part-time pay slinging coffee. You'd be better off hiring a real live servant to bring beer and popcorn."

Taylor sighed and put down the Playboy, and the lamp lifted away. "I guess we'd better get down to business." Into the air, he inquired, "Surveillance, where do I keep the safe?"

"I can't tell you," replied the voice of his father's long-time girlfriend from the bookshelves where her camera-eyes were probably watching them.

He exchanged alarmed glances with his friend. *Have we been found out?* he wondered in a panic. It was almost impossible to pose the question again, but steeling himself, he asked, "Who am I?"

"You are David Hamilton," she replied cordially.

Feeling himself sag with relief, he asked, "Then why won't you tell me where the safe is?"

"I can't."

"*Why* can't you?"

"Because I don't know."

"You . . . oh come on. You're *surveillance* for God's sake!"

"Don't you remember? You blocked the information. The location of the safe is in my system, of course. I am blocked from accessing it, though."

"Shit!" Taylor exclaimed.

"Should I inform cleaning?" she asked.

"It's an expression." To Shawn he explained, "It makes sense, I guess. It's unlikely that hackers could get into surveillance, but the Robot-man can't take any chances."

His friend shrugged. "And, robots don't lie."

Her naive question sparked an idea, however.

"I changed my mind," he called. "I do want cleaning."

"You betcha," she enthused.

Taylor winced. It was an archaic expression his father's girlfriend liked to use.

Seconds later, a whirring sound announced the arrival of a shiny chrome clean-bot.

"I was expecting something more exotic," Shawn commented, watching the familiar little domed machine roll up. "—something without, like, wheels. Heck, my uncle has one of these."

"Yeah, but can his find a flea in the carpet and then identify its sub-species?"

"Yoo hab summoned zee cleaning service," the diminutive bot declared in a thick German accent.

Shawn laughed out loud. "That's rich! I was expecting a Hispanic voice."

"My genius father never does what you expect." To the Teutonic machine, he said, "Do you know where my safe is?"

"Of co-urse."

"Take me there."

"Das ist verboten!"

Taylor nodded. He'd expected that. "Fine. Tell you what, mine commandant, I need you to clean up some coffee that I spilled."

"It vood be my plea-sure. Vere iz zee shpill?"

"Next to my safe."

"Wunderbar. I shall get right on it."

Taylor waved to his friend, and they followed the unperturbed little clean-bot out of the great living hall, through a long, lavishly decorated dining room and kitchen large enough to serve the Hotel del Coronado, out a side door, and when they emerged into a screened porch furnished with white wicker, the Deutsche-bot stopped.

"I see no coffee," the machine protested.

"Yeah," Taylor agreed, glancing around, but finding only arrays of plush cushions festooning a setting out of Casablanca. "Er, the spill is right *next* to the safe."

Clean-bot seemed to consider this. "Zees is most unfortunate, but I must ask for further assistance. On vich side of ze safe is ze shpill?"

"Uh, the closest side, I guess."

He glanced at Shawn and shrugged.

Commandant janitor moved five inches towards Taylor and complained, "I shtill don't zee it!" The little storm trooper sounded truly vexed.

"Oh, never mind. I guess it already dried."

The domed clean-machine sat silently, brooding a moment, and then declared, "Zere is nussing more I can do here," before zipping away with a distinctly haughty whir.

Taylor got down on his hands and knees on the tile floor, and saw it. What appeared to be a small hole accidentally chipped out of the edge of one of the large square plates seemed to have no bottom. He curled his finger inside, and pulled, and the tile tilted smoothly up on hidden hinges, revealing beneath it the door of a safe buried under the floor facing up.

"Well, look at that!" Shawn declared approvingly. "The back door to Fort Knox."

"We're only after the ring, you know," Taylor reproved, tapping out the access code on the safe's keypad. "We're not thieves."

The safe beeped and flashed a red light. "That was the main gate code," Jimmy Durante's voice growled helpfully.

"Shit," Taylor hissed.

"You need that Nazis char-man back?" Durante asked.

"No," Taylor replied, sitting back and wrapping his arms around his knees.

"You were hoping it was the same code, weren't you?" Shawn asked.

"I should have known my father wouldn't be that sloppy."

"Maybe the surveillance woman can give it to you," he suggested without much enthusiasm.

"Oh, she probably knows, but I'm sure she's not telling."

"It's worth a try."

"Surveillance!" Taylor called into the porch.

"Yes, David?"

"Do you know the combination to the safe?"

"Of course."

"Would you tell me?"

"I'm sorry, I can't do that—"

"Let me guess: your access to that information is blocked."

"You are indeed a genius, David."

Shawn's eyes widened in surprise.

"Don't be impressed," Taylor cautioned, "my father probably programmed that as a canned response. He's that kind of jerk."

Taylor reminded himself that he'd better watch what he said. Surveillance was likely recording everything.

She probably records any time there's activity in the house, he thought idly.

He gasped and looked at his friend.

"What?" Shawn asked, alarmed.

"That's it!"

"What's it?"

"Surveillance!" he called again.

"Yes, David."

"Play back the monitored sound from the last time I used the safe."

"Do you want the audio from each room, or just this one?"

"Just this one."

To Shawn, he explained, "Maybe I can work out which buttons he pushed from the tones—wait! Surveillance, do you have video for this room?"

"Of course, David."

"Play the video of the last time I used the safe—just this area."

Each room of the house had a flat screen attached to a wall, and this one burst to life with an angled view from the far corner. They watched as Taylor's father walked in knelt down, and lifted the tile. His body blocked the view.

"Do you have another angle? I want to see the keypad."

"Isn't that, like, a little obvious?" Shawn whispered into his ear.

"You keep letting their apparent language skills fool you. They really are just dumb machines."

The view changed to the other corner of the room, and the keypad was clearly visible as the Robot-man punched out the code, then lifted up the safe door.

"Play that back, and zoom in on the keypad. Go slowly. I want to see what buttons he pushes."

The view expanded dizzily, and a huge finger pressed methodically on buttons the size of the cushions lying about.

Shawn chuckled and shook his head in amazement.

"Ah, got it," Taylor crowed triumphantly.

Seconds later, he lifted the door of the safe, and Durante welcomed him by lighting the interior.

Inside were just two boxes. Taylor lifted one out and opened it. It was stuffed with bundles of thousand-dollar bills.

"Oh my God," Shawn moaned, reaching out to reverently caress one bundle. "I've never actually touched a grand-spot."

"And that's all you're going to do tonight."

He held the box up and called out as he slipped the top back on, "See, Dad? We didn't take any!"

He lay the heavy package aside and reached down to pull out the other box. With luck this would be full of jewelry, one piece of which he hoped would be the engagement ring his father had given his mother more than two decades before. The small world of celebrity San Diego waited with bated breath for the Robot-man to ask his girlfriend to marry him, and Taylor's mom was sure the bastard was going to offer the nubile ditz that same ring.

But not if he could help it.

The second box was weighty, but didn't feel like individual pieces. It felt solid. He pulled off the top and stared at the contents.

"What the hell is it?" Shawn asked over his shoulder.

"I . . . I don't know."

It looked like a long, dark skinny turd curled neatly into the box. Coil after coil wrapped back and forth and around itself so that the serpentine tube filled every last cubic millimeter of the space inside.

The turd lifted its head and spoke. "What's going on?" it asked in a quiet, beguiling male voice.

Flush with the rough textured skin were what must have been eyes—smooth impenetrable glossy patches that seemed to see everything while looking at nothing.

It wasn't a turd. It was a snake!

"Who are you?" it asked, lifting more of its length up and turning the head in a slow arc.

"Um, you don't know?" Taylor asked.

"No," it replied simply.

"Surveillance hasn't . . . told you?"

"I have no contact with other devices."

"I'm . . . well, I'm David."

The snake paused immobile a moment. Taylor felt the hair prickling on his arms.

"David Hamilton?" the snake asked.

"Yeah—the owner of this house."

"Hello, David. It's good to see you again."

Taylor exhaled with relief.

"So, like," Shawn muttered, "what is it?"

"I have no idea. But it must." The tapered head turned to him and he asked it, "What are you?"

"An appliance, of course."

Taylor was used to household devices talking without lips, but this robot serpent looked too much like an actual animal. It was disconcerting that no mouth uttered the words.

"But, for what purpose?"

The snake's gentle voice was patient, calming. "General utility. My shape conveys function."

"Scaring birds, maybe?"

"Perhaps," the snake replied agreeably. "Or cleaning out drains, for example."

"You . . . go down drains? Like, *all* drains?"

The hovering head dipped slightly in a demure nod. "I have not performed that task yet, so I am still pristinely clean," it added, seeming to read Taylor's mind.

"I see. Uh, that's good, I guess."

"As you taught me, I am also handy at retrieving items that have rolled under the bed."

Taylor wondered uneasily whether the reptilian appliance was being sarcastic.

"Why does . . . why do I keep you in the safe?"

The snake paused as though letting the inappropriateness of him of all people asking the question register. "Why, because I am valuable, of course."

"Right. Of course. And, uh, why particularly are you valuable?"

"David, as you yourself explained, I am the first viable prototype of my class of appliance. The competition would pay a fortune to get hold of me."

"Right. Of course."

What competition? Taylor wondered. He didn't know his father even had any.

"Hey," Shawn whispered. "We should be going. What if your father . . . er, you come home early?"

He sighed. "Yeah. I guess so."

"No ring," his friend observed sympathetically.

Taylor snorted. "With my luck, he probably gave it to the little wench just tonight."

Shawn picked up the box of cash lovingly. "It's a shame we have to leave empty-handed."

"You're not thieves, remember?" the snake reproved.

Buried down there in the safe, it must have been listening to him, Taylor realized.

He snatched the box from his friend and tossed it back into Durante's gut. "No, we're not."

The featureless glaze of the snake's eye coverings stared at him. For as long as humans could put words to the thought, the legless reptiles had carried a reputation for cold calculation. Even the Bible had enlisted one as a metaphor for calculated persuasion.

The inscrutable eyes seemed to dare him.

Very well.

"We're not thieves," Taylor reiterated, placing the palm of his free hand over the snake's head and gently forcing it to coil back into the box. "We're just trying to get back stolen goods from someone who is."

"Place me back in the safe . . . David," the nano-machine drain cleaner directed calmly as Taylor slipped the box cover back on and headed off towards the kitchen.

"Wait!" Shawn called. "What the heck . . . we can't just . . . arghh!"

Taylor heard Shawn slam the safe closed, followed by the tile cover, and his friend caught up with him back in the great living hall. "Look," Shawn hissed through tight lips, "if that lamp costs more than I can afford, this snake prototype must be worth a real fortune."

"We're not stealing it. We're holding it in trade."

From the box in his hands came the muffled voice of reason. "Would a jury agree with you?"

"Shut up!"

The next instant they were walking through darkness.

"Oh, Christ," Taylor muttered, exasperated. "Full lights!"

The voluminous hall blazed with blinding radiance as though the sun had burst forth. Lighting-boy had literally turned every light in the house on.

This was probably costing a fortune in electricity itself.

Good.

Outside, the night was all the darker for the contrast, but in the near distance, tortured tires squealed as they hung on desperately to a curve, then, roaring closer, wailed in despair, seeming surprised themselves that they managed to stop the Lamborghini at the top of the driveway.

"Oh, shit!" Shawn cried. "It's your father!"

The gate was sliding open.

"Come on," Shawn pleaded, tugging at Taylor's arm. "We can't just stand here!"

Taylor's heart was pounding, but he felt a stubborn resolve. He was rooted to the spot by ten years of simmering resentment, listening to his mom's mantra of abandonment.

"Where would you go?" he barked, shaking off Shawn's arm. "This place is a walled fortress."

The yellow muscle of finely machined Italian metal screeched to a stop in front of them, the doors lifted like a bird extending its wings for takeoff, and his father slid out, his face no more threatening beneath the neatly trimmed beard, but no less intense, than usual.

The owner of the house they'd robbed skipped up the steps, glanced at Shawn, who shamefully slipped off the Groucho glasses, and turned to meet Taylor's eyes. "You look like an idiot."

"I look like *you*," he snapped back.

But he did suddenly feel foolish, and ripped off the costume beard, tossing it away.

"I think you have something of mine," his father noted casually, nodding at the box in Taylor's hand.

"How did you know we were here?"

"Your hostage called me when he heard you trying to get into the safe." With more volume, he called, "Prototype Three—to me!"

Taylor felt the box jiggle in his hand, and watched the top lift and fall away as the robot's head emerged. Frozen by the eerie bold faculty of the thing, Taylor stood motionless as the artificial serpent spiraled along his arm, around his torso, and then slithered along the paving stones to the waiting hand. The machine's creator lifted it so that it could curl around his neck and shoulders as it might a tree in the forest.

Is it still a machine when there are no distinct moving parts? he wondered.

"It knew who I was all along," Taylor murmured as though the other two weren't even there.

His father lifted the brim of his cap and scratched his forehead. "From what I heard, it was pretty obvious."

Taylor shook his head slowly in protest. "Robots don't lie!"

His dad, the Robot-man, snorted and pulled his cap back down, as though embarrassed for his son. "Why do you think that is?"

"Because . . ." he looked to Shawn who just stared at him, trying to be invisible by force of will. "I guess they're just not smart enough."

His father nodded. His progeny apparently wasn't a complete idiot. "Did you ever consider that this might be by design?"

Taylor waited, unwilling to answer a question that was obviously rhetorical.

"Americans would never accept intelligent appliances," he continued, glancing at Shawn who cringed at the attention. "They'd feel threatened. Our market economy depends on confident consumers. For its own survival, our culture convinces us that we're each golden little gods. Hell, everybody has a pile of trophies to prove it."

Taylor was used to these unbidden mini-lectures. Like this one, they were often an observation on some aspect of the consummate stupidity of the masses. And now, like the times before, Taylor felt tossed in along with the sheep.

"But not this one," Shawn blurted.

They both looked at him, and he seemed horrified at his outburst.

"I mean," he stammered, "the snake is smart—it can lie."

Taylor looked at his father, who returned his gaze impassively.

The reason seemed obvious. "It's for the CIA," Taylor guessed.

The stone face never faltered, but his father's eyes were not the immutable electronic receptors of his reptilian creation. Using his human intuition, Taylor saw an affirmation.

"It would be, like, the perfect spy," Shawn whispered. "It could sneak around anywhere."

The Robot-man yanked his cap down farther over his eyes and walked past them. "Get the hell out of here before I call the police."

The relief on his friend's face was that of a man reprieved from the guillotine. An instant later Shawn was sprinting away down the driveway.

Taylor hesitated. The same human intuition had heard something behind the gruff dismissal.

As though the robot snake whispered as much into his ear, Taylor's father stopped and turned. Two sets of eyes studied Taylor, one a mechanical surveillance without dimension, the other glittering with the complexity of a human soul.

His father reached inside his coat and took out a jewelry box, which he handed to him. "It's time your mother had this," he said, turning back to his brilliantly lit house.

Taylor looked at the rounded felt top. He knew what was inside. "Your girlfriend turned you down, didn't she?" he said.

His father spun and glared at him a moment, then relaxed. "I didn't ask." A tiny smile turned up the corners of his mouth. "I could read the cards—I decided not to play a bad hand."

The Robot-man seemed perplexed a moment, then raised one eyebrow. "Did your mother ever tell you why I have her ring?"

Taylor shrugged. "She just said that you wouldn't give it back."

He nodded knowingly, and then shook his head in exasperation. "She jammed it into my pocket when I left. She told me that she didn't want it back until I was ready to come with it."

He shook his head again at the absurdity, and turned back to his mansion.

Taylor started down the stairs, but stopped. "The lighting," he called, turning back.

The Robot-man paused in the open doorway and looked at him.

"The voice of the lighting system—is that mine?"

His father watched him a moment. The head of the artificial snake, the lying robot, swayed slowly under the guidance of its positional algorithms. Its expression was a complete void, but its master's was that of a father gazing fondly at his son.

The Robot-man stepped inside the painfully bright interior and closed the door.

The Chosen Ones

"Aliens?" Cameron repeated into the phone, annoyed with his friend. "Space aliens?"

"Yeah," Byron enthused. "They're here, and I think you're a perfect candidate. You need to come over, like, now."

Actually, Byron wasn't really his friend—more of an acquaintance, and a reluctantly acknowledged one at that. If he were an actual friend, Cameron might have been excited, or perhaps amused. As it was, he was just annoyed. Nobody took the guy seriously. Cameron picked up a good sci-fi book when he had time, but Byron was obsessed—pathologically. He still lived with his parents, and since they were mega-rich and he an only-child, probably would for life.

"Nah. I have to work on my applications, and Jennie may be calling—"

"Tristan is coming."

Whoa. That changed things. Tristan had been his academic rival throughout their graduate program. Cameron wouldn't expect him to be snookered into one of Byron's delusional fantasies. Hell,

Tristan had already been accepted as a doctoral candidate in Stanford's physics program.

"What do they look like?" Cameron asked, trying to sound only casually interested.

"They're, like, about six inches long, and they fly—they look like big humming birds."

"How do you know they're aliens, and *not* big humming birds?"

"They told me."

"They told you."

"Of course. What kind of aliens would come all the way to Earth and not be able to, like, even talk?"

"I'll be right over. Keep an eye on them. If they fly away, try to—"

"They're sitting here on my table. They're not going anywhere until they talk to you. They want to know if you want to be a spaceship pilot."

Cameron sighed. "Are you sure Tristan is coming?"

He heard a voice in the background. It sounded like Alvin the chipmunk from the tired novelty Christmas song. "Tell him Mothership has passed perihelion behind sun long time, and we must meet in twenty-eight thousand seconds or be left behind," it said.

"I'm on my way!" Cameron shouted, almost dropping the phone as he jammed it into his pocket and ran out.

It was still probably a hoax, but if there was the slightest chance that anybody was going to be a spaceship pilot, it was going to be him, and not that over-achiever Tristan.

ж ж ж

Apparently it would be both.

The aliens needed two pilots, and as they put it, waggling their leathery little wings provocatively as they sat on their haunches on Byron's table, "Not easy find pilots caliber as us."

Cameron still had a hard time believing what perched proud and confident before him, even though he could come up with no better explanation for three parchment-skinned flying lizards with tiny monkey heads who could talk, albeit using toddler grammar. Byron had explained that they translated their name as the Dangerous Wilies, as in wily. Their ship sat in Byron's backyard. It looked like a Volkswagen Bug minus the wheels and windows. Cameron found it somehow disquieting that there were dents in it. The Salvadoran landscape workers buzzing their way along the ten-foot hedges around the perimeter glanced at it apprehensively every now and then, but had learned long ago to ignore the idiosyncrasies of their benefactors. With wealth came the prerogative to be eccentric.

"Tristan and Cameron are, like, Greek gods," Byron assured. "They get, you know, like straight A's and are real athletic. Tristan mountain-bikes and swims, and Cameron can run—"

"If wanted Greeks," the Dangerous Wilies' apparent leader interrupted, "would go to Greece. Want Americans."

"It's an expression," Cameron explained. "He means that we're—that he *thinks* that we're superior humans."

Tristan shrugged. "No need for false modesty."

"Need pilots who learn quickly—nimble hands and minds—adapt foreign environment," the alien instructed. "Also, not weep loneliness when away home," he added. "No babies."

"Why Americans?" Cameron asked.

He was split down the middle. Half of him, the half that had brought him to California to go to grad school instead of his undergraduate alma mater Penn State, was ready to climb into the Space Beetle and fly off to a fantastic future in the future. The other half, though, the half who couldn't get up the nerve to tell Jennie they were through, was supremely suspicious of aliens who looked like Wizard of Oz characters offering up comic book roles.

"Americans always win," the alien replied.

"Like, wars?"

"Wars. Battles. Baseball. Heroine's heart."

"So, it's space fighter pilots you want."

Cameron wasn't going to explain that it was Americans making the movies they were probably intercepting. To the scriptwriter goes the victor.

The Dangerous Wilies glanced at each other. "Fighter pilots, yes."

"So, why don't you go find an actual American fighter pilot?"

"Tried. Always drunk. Always swatting at us. Called us ugly flying turds."

This was the main reason Cameron made sure he got good grades. His family was poor, and he *never* wanted to default to military service.

"Why Byron?" he asked.

"Byron not go. He too whippersnapper—"

"No. I mean why did you come here, to his house?"

"Big privacy. People gawk."

'Big privacy'—*that* Byron had, or at least his parents did. The grounds must be five acres, surrounded by a nearly impenetrable wall.

"They were uneasy about the immigrant landscape workers," Byron explained. "At first they wanted me to lock them in a room. I explained about them, that they'd be too scared to tell anybody for fear of the attention."

"Byron also easy mark," the alien added. "Believes fiction stories."

"Diplomacy doesn't seem very high on their list," Cameron commented.

Byron just shrugged. He seemed tickled pink just to have them here.

"Let's cut to the chase," Tristan said, grasping Cameron's arm to maneuver him out of the way. "What exactly would our status be? Would our ranks coming in be First Lieutenants? Or, maybe Captains? We have Master's Degrees—that should count for something."

The Dangerous Wilies exchanged more cloistered glances. They flicked wing tips in what Cameron took to be assent. "Majors," the leader proclaimed. "We be Generals. Superior."

"I'd like to know why they don't fly their fighter ships themselves," Cameron suggested from behind Tristan.

His rival looked at him, and then turned back to the aliens. The three of them sat there a minute, then, apparently accepting that they couldn't just ignore the question, the leader said, "We too important."

"That makes sense," Tristan concurred.

"So, flying fighter spaceships is dangerous," Cameron suggested, looking over Tristan's shoulder.

The three little Dangerous Wilies sat immobile, their wee wings twitching randomly. "Okay," the leader finally replied. "Like this. We no capable."

"You mean, you're not able to fly the fighters?" Cameron pressed, nudging Tristan aside, who resisted so that they scuffled silently a few seconds before Cameron put his hands up in truce, and they stood tensely side-by-side.

The alien leader's wings stuck straight out like yucca leaves. "Able, of course. Not *capable*."

"Seems perfectly reasonable," Tristan said. "After all, you wouldn't expect an Air Force General to fly a fighter—"

"Actually, I would," Cameron cut in. "At least, the Air Force General would be capable."

The leader's extended wings vibrated. "Okay. Like this. Fighter controls built for big body."

"The ships were designed for *humans*?" Cameron asked.

"No. That silly. No one know humans 'til now. Built for big body, two arms."

"They were designed for a race similar to humans?"

"Similar in body. Smarter in head. Big smarter."

"Well, duh! They know how to build interstellar space ships."

"Time short. Must go. You two acceptable."

The leader jumped into the air and the room was filled with the frantic burr of beating wings. The other two crouched, ready to follow, when Cameron shouted, "Hold on!" and the leader sank back to the table.

"What now?" the Dangerous Wily complained.

"Are you nuts! You think we'll follow you to go gallivanting off to some space opera stellar war like you're some kind of alien Peter Pan? We don't work that way."

"I would," Tristan declared.

"Shut up. Look, if they need fighter pilots so badly, it must mean that they expect a fight. I'd like to know a little bit about the person—the thing—that's going to try its best to kill me." To the alien, he demanded, "Well?"

The wings were jerking nervously again. "Always good to be prepared."

"I don't buy it. I think you're expecting trouble."

"Okay. Like this. Another people mad. Want Mother Ship. But they weak. Stupid. No problem. No worry."

"Uh, uh. I still don't buy it. If they were really that stupid, you wouldn't need us—we're not 'big smarter' either, remember?"

"I don't know why you have to be so contrary," Tristan sniffed. "You act as though you don't—"

"Will you shut *up* already!" Cameron shouted.

"Maybe one enough," the Dangerous Wilies leader concluded. "We go now with just you," he said, looking at Tristan.

Cameron's classmate nodded agreeably.

"Wait!" Cameron cried. He wasn't sure why he was bothering. "Look, Tristan, this is crazy. Think about it. We're talking about different species at war here. What're the chances that the weapon technologies are going to be anywhere near comparable? What're the chances? Even if the two species had developed at the same time—in itself absurdly unlikely—they wouldn't necessarily share the same level of advancement. Think British guns against Aborigine spears, only multiplied a thousand-fold. Either they're the Aborigines, in which case Big Dangerous Willy Wonka here wouldn't need you, or *you* are, and you're serving yourself up as cosmic hors d'oeuvres."

For the first time, Tristan looked reflective.

"No!" the alien leader squeaked. "Technologies same."

"The same?" Cameron repeated as a challenge.

"Exactly same."

It's wings jutted out again like sea urchin spines. Cameron was beginning to see a pattern.

"How can they be exactly the same? That's impossible."

"Not big smart, indeed. Built by same *people*!"

That stopped Cameron. "These people . . . they *stole* fighter space ships from you? Now they're going to use them against you?"

The leader's wings collapsed back against its body, jerking and shaking. "Yes. Stole ships. Use them against we."

"Because they also want to steal your Mother Ship."

"Yes!" The wings shivered as though the creature was cold. "You help us."

Cameron and Tristan glanced at each other.

"One more question," Cameron said. "You obviously couldn't have built the fighter ships—"

"We big smart!" the leader protested. "We think way bigger than you—"

"That may be. I'm simply stating the obvious. Why would you build ships you couldn't use?"

The wings reached out straight. "Okay. Like this. We not only species on Mother Ship. Other species big, big smart. Big, big smarter than you. Big."

"I don't doubt it," Cameron muttered watching the leader. He thought he was maybe getting the picture here.

"Other species our friends," the leader of the Dangerous Wilies crowed. "We live harmony."

"Well," Tristan proclaimed, shoving Cameron aside so that he could stand in front of the aliens. "I've heard enough. I'm ready to defend you from these invaders. It would be an honor to be the first human to join the cosmic fold."

"Suit yourself," Cameron said. "Maybe they'll hang a medal around your neck."

I should let the twerp go, he thought as the three Dangerous Wilies took to the air, sounding like a squadron of vacuum cleaners. The human gene pool would be the better for it.

Ah hell.

"Hey, Tristan!" he shouted above the drone. "Don't worry about your slaves! Byron and I will take care of them for you!"

"What the hell are you talking about!" Tristan shouted back.

Byron looked puzzled, trying to remember if Tristan had ever told him about them.

The three aliens had backed up and away, and were now facing them from near the ceiling as though a triplet of giant bees ready to attack.

"Humans keep not slaves anymore," the leader protested. His voice seemed to resonate with the hum so that it sounded larger, more apropos of something called a Dangerous Wily.

"You've obviously been watching old news! Graduates of higher education are now allowed to own people who've had their homes foreclosed. Tristan bought five from the bank!"

"He's lying!" Tristan shouted, his arms folded across his chest in defiance.

Cameron carefully held his arms outstretched. "Who is lying?" he asked the leader. Cameron nodded knowingly at Tristan.

The alien Dangerous Wily hovered, eyeing them both a moment, then turned and flew out the door. The other two followed, but a moment later, the leader appeared again and called to Byron.

"What in good God's name are you doing?" Tristan growled at Cameron as Byron trotted out after the Wilies to confer next to their Space Beetle. He gave Cameron a shove.

"Saving your ugly ass!" he replied, giving his nemesis a bigger shove in return. "You don't get it, do you?"

"Get what? That you blew the best adventure I'll ever see?"

"You think Kunta Kinte gave his mom a kiss and assured her he was going off on a great adventure when he was captured in Africa?"

"What is *with* you and slaves all of a sudden?"

"What do you think the Dangerous Wilies are?"

Tristan shook his head in angered annoyance. His confidence in the righteous justification of his anger seemed to be wavering, though.

"They—are—slaves!" Cameron shouted. Geez, how could a Stanford doctoral candidate be so thick? "It all makes sense. Their masters stole the Mother Ship, and the rightful owners are coming to get it back. That's why the fighter ships are the same. They make up this big, scary name—Dangerous Wilies—to cover their shame."

Tristan looked downright dumbfounded. "How . . . how do you conclude all this?"

"Didn't you notice? Their wings are all weak and shivery when they're lying, and bold and straight when they tell the truth. That's how I convinced them that you own slaves. They instinctively interpret the positions of our arms as though they were wings. Didn't you hear how they talked about the 'other species' on the Mother Ship? 'Big, big smart—we live in harmony.' Cut me a break. That's ingrained cow-towing if I ever heard it."

Byron appeared in the doorway all flushed. "They conferred with the Mother Ship. They've changed plans."

"You mean they've gotten different instructions from their masters," Cameron countered.

Byron looked at him as though he'd just spoken in French. "They're not taking either of you," he continued, seeming deeply disappointed.

Through the open doorway, Cameron saw the aliens herding the three landscape workers into the Space Beetle. It was a tight fit, and the last one barely squeezed in.

"Holy shit!" Cameron shouted, running outside, but it was too late. With an ear-splitting whine, the overloaded planet shuttle heaved itself off the ground, wavered, slid sideways into the gazebo adding another dent to the mix, then slowly rose up and away. The whine faded into the blue sky, and all that was left was the abandoned hedge-trimming tools lying forlornly around on the ground.

"They said that the Salvadorans were better candidates," Byron explained huffing and puffing up next to him. "They said that these guys were already used to living far from home, and were less likely to be big babies."

Cameron nodded. "Probably right."

Tristan came up appearing sheepish.

"You know," Cameron went on, "considering that they're going to have to come to grips with a whole new technology in a whole new environment, well, I think they took the better crew after all."

"But they're going to be . . . slaves," Tristan objected, looking horrified.

Cameron shrugged and headed back towards the house. "Who knows, maybe they'll turn the tables—maybe return to Earth as heroes with the rightful owners of the Mother Ship."

"Yeah!" Tristan called after him. "And maybe there's really a Santa Claus."

"Nobody's proven there isn't," he said quietly to himself.

Then he spread his arms wide to demonstrate the truth of that.

The Shoes of Moses

Character

"The Waldorf," Jamee said, stepping into the booth a block from her apartment in Boulder. She then quickly added, "San Diego," remembering she'd been to Manhattan just the week before.

"Restaurant, or pastry factory?" the booth queried.

"I'm going to a factory dressed like this?" she asked, lifting her hands and rolling her eyes at the old woman waiting next in line. The woman looked bored, and didn't react.

"Waldorf restaurant," the booth chimed with no trace of sarcasm.

The deep dusk of the Colorado mountains was instantly replaced by a blinding sun hovering over the moored sailboats of San Diego harbor. Jamee stepped out, and a man walked in behind her and barked, "Seventeen"—his speed-dial for some oft-visited location.

She patted herself and looked at both of her bare arms before glancing around for the restaurant. Her friends laughed at this eccentricity. She knew it was a silly thing to worry about, but it was still a fact that every bit of the Jamee of two minutes ago was still in Boulder. Random pieces of her were now walking out of the booth on her street as maybe the nose of a man, and the kneecap of a little girl.

Okay, it wasn't that simple. Still, every fragment of the new San Diego her, over the last hour, had belonged to any number of other users of this booth. A boyfriend in high school had patiently explained that even if she never stepped into another booth, ten years down the road her body would consist of completely different molecules, as her cells wore out and new ones grew.

It was best not to think about the whole thing. Nobody else did.

She found that the Waldorf was surrounded by small trees in large pots. It looked expensive. The guy was either well off, or trying to impress her. Her booth-fear was replaced by a more prosaic preoccupation: was she about to spend two hours with the father of her children, or an insufferable jerk? On the other hand, what if he was Prince Charming, and didn't like her? She wasn't fooling herself; "attractive" wouldn't be the first adjective he'd mentally log.

She suddenly wondered if it had been a mistake to choose the non-visual track of the dating service. It had seemed romantic in an old-fashioned sort of way at the time.

"Balls!" she snorted and stormed off towards the potted trees. A man and woman, both in formal wear, turned and gave her a surprised look, and she shrugged. She noticed that the man was wearing dress gloves. Sleek hand coverings had gone out of general style months ago, but black ones were still considered an essential part of a man's formal outfit.

The Waldorf's lobby was a whole jungle of plants. She didn't see a maitre-console, and decided that the man with the funny uniform standing at the podium was serving as the human version. This *was* a fancy place.

"Jamee to meet Bob," she said to the uniformed man a bit tentatively.

She half expected him to raise his eyebrows and say, "So?" Instead, he nodded and purred, "Very good, miss; follow me," before gliding off through the sea of tables.

She followed, thinking, *who would have named their child "Bob" anyway?* He must have had a difficult time with it in grade school. It was hard to imagine Prince Charming with a first name like Bob. Why not Scrooge, or Ishmael?

She felt her heart pounding. The internal banter was just an attempt to distract herself. If her friends were here, she'd be babbling away a mile a minute.

But what if he doesn't like me?

The maitre-man suddenly stopped and held out his hand, as though offering the guy seated at a small table for sale.

Bob wasn't so bad. Late thirties, maybe. A face she could live with. Fit body—muscled shoulders. She couldn't tell if he was natural or induced.

He stood up, scraping his chair across the floor behind him. "Bob," he said, smiling and holding his hand out. He too wore evening gloves, but his looked old and tired, as though constant, road-weary companions.

She looked at the extended hand a moment before realizing that he was offering it. Why? To kiss her fingers? That would be in sync with the nostalgic opulence of the restaurant. Maybe he just wanted to shake her hand. She slowly stuck hers out, and he grasped it gently and shook it up and down.

"Pleased to meet you, Jamee," he said, apparently now waiting for her to sit down before he did so himself.

Boy, this guy really was a Bob—straight out of the last century. Maybe he was one of those people that froze themselves hoping for a future cure for their terminal illness.

She sat down slowly, watching him. He waited until she was seated, then pulled his chair back with another loud clatter and sat down himself. She saw that the people at other tables were staring at them. *The guy's name is Bob, for God's sake*, she wanted to tell them, but they turned back to their food. Her companion asked if she'd had a good trip.

She shrugged and smiled. "The booth worked."

What trip? she thought. She'd walked maybe a hundred steps between her apartment and here.

"Good," he said, nodding knowingly. Like the booth itself, he didn't seem to catch the sarcasm. "We take them for granted, don't we?"

"Actually, I don't," she countered. "My friends think I'm paranoid, but I get the heebie-jeebies every time I imagine my body being torn apart and instantly reconstructed a thousand miles away from the parts of other people's bodies."

Bob smiled condescendingly, it seemed to her. "Others' bodies only in the sense that the individual atoms once comprised them."

"What other sense is there?"

It was Bob's turn to shrug. He picked up the menu.

She realized that he might be feeling insulted. "I keep thinking what would happen if the booth runs short of some key element," she said, trying to pull him back. "Like potassium or something. I'd be dead before I knew what happened."

He put down the menu and gave her another of those condescending smiles. "The sending booth won't start the teardown if the receiving booth isn't ready."

"I know, but things break."

"Booths are the most reliable machines ever built by man," he assured.

Jamee was going to reiterate that her fear wasn't rational, but he went on.

"Did you ever consider how booth operation is similar to how cars were rented a hundred years ago?"

She lifted her shoulders. She had only the vaguest idea that people could even rent cars then—mostly from movies of the period. "In both cases you pay by the klick?" she offered.

"That's true," he said, "but I was thinking how each relies on a random pattern of use by their customers."

She shook her head, perplexed. This was a pretty bizarre way to get acquainted. Weren't they supposed to talk about their families, or whether they liked cats?

"The automobile rental companies wanted to avoid moving their cars from one location to another," he went on. "Instead, they depended on their one-way customers to move the cars for them. The ideal was to have exactly as many cars being driven away as arriving."

Jamee nodded, trying to be congenial. "I see. If everybody in Boulder decided to come to San Diego, the booths here would run out of elements. There has to be as many people transporting away from San Diego, leaving their elements behind."

Bob smiled. It was a smile she remembered from grade school teachers when she got an answer right. *How can I hate that smile now*, she thought, *when I so craved it back then?*

"You seem to know a lot about booths," she observed. "Do you design them?"

"A design engineer? No. That's not nearly as interesting a profession as most people think—mostly just worrying about a lot of esoteric details."

Did she detect sour grapes? "Maybe a historian, then?"

He brightened at this. "By interest only. No formal education."

She sighed. "I like a game of twenty questions as well as anybody . . ."

Bob nodded in understanding. "Sorry. I'm a field support technician for Gee-TRIC."

She'd heard that name before. "Global Transporter Innovations Corporation," she announced a bit proudly, realizing she was still, after all these years, working for that smile. "They build booths," she added.

"Largest manufacturer in the world. You probably used one coming here."

Bob sat looking at her.

"You fix booths," she said after a few seconds.

He blushed. "As the mundane part of my job, yes. But I also install and test upgrades. I've testified in court as an expert witness."

"That booths are the most reliable machines ever built by man?"

He blushed deeper. "A civil suit. A woman lost a foot in a freak accident."

"She lost her *foot?*"

Bob gave one solemn nod. "Both a primary and backup circuit failed at the same time. A one-in-a-million chance."

She didn't want to hear this. She wanted him to explain how the booths were absolutely, totally infallible. "I never heard about it."

"Of course not. Gee-TRIC wields a lot of clout. They indirectly own I-CNN and W-BLOG, and have influence over all the other major net-news companies. You'd have to dig deep to find the stories. There were twenty-nine booth-related deaths last year, you know."

"People *died?*"

Bob wrinkled his brow in consternation. "Booths are used over a hundred million times every day. Twenty-nine deaths in a year is virtually a zero percentage."

"Not for the people who died."

"More people died from swallowing condoms."

"I've never put a condom in my mouth, but I use a booth every day . . . wait a second; you said the woman lost her foot in a million-to-one accident. If booths are used a hundred million times every day—"

"It's just an expression. Okay, a billion-to-one chance."

She looked at him. "That means the same accident happens every ten days."

Bob rolled his eyes. "A trillion-to-one—whatever. You might as well worry about getting hit by a meteor."

As a matter of fact, she had worried about that for a couple of weeks when she was twelve.

"It looks like we're getting off on the wrong foot," she suggested. "Maybe we should change the subject."

A grin spread across Bob's face. "That's probably what that woman was thinking when she stepped out of the booth."

Jamee stared at him.

"Get it? She got off 'on the wrong foot'?"

Jamee wagged her head. "I get it, I get it. Isn't that a bit morbid?"

Bob didn't reply. Instead, with lips pressed tight, he picked up the menu again and studied it.

This was going to hell fast.

"I drove a car last year," she said in an attempt to assuage his hurt feelings.

He looked up at her with raised eyebrows.

"In South Africa," she added.

His face drooped in disappointment. "You're talking about the so-called Twentieth Century Exposition."

"That's right—were you there?"

"I didn't bother. Those were hardly automobiles. Most of them were built after 2030."

"It looked like a car to me."

"Did you use a steering wheel?"

"Of course not! I would've killed somebody."

"So, you didn't really drive the car. You were merely a passenger."

"I told it where to go," she said, feeling poutful, like the tables had been turned.

Bob lifted his left eyebrow in a skeptical question.

She picked up her menu and gave it all her attention. Two could play that game.

Yikes! She noticed the prices for the first time. She hoped he'd offer to pay. He had suggested this place, after all. In case he didn't, though, she decided to have a tofu casserole, even though they advertised that their beef was real meat.

"I've driven a car—a real one," Bob remarked casually as he scanned down his menu.

"Really?" she asked, pretending interest. It wouldn't hurt her to be gracious. "Where?"

"Uzbekistan. Booths are privately owned there. This old fellow had a dozen, and kept an ancient Honda SUV that he used to get to the booths when they broke down. He said his grandfather bought it used in '25. It must be one of the last surviving manual cars, other than in the Smithsonian. He wouldn't tell me where he gets his gas."

She found herself intrigued, despite herself. "I never thought about that."

She glanced up from her menu to find him looking at her. "I mean, how do you get to a booth when it's not working? It's sort of the chicken or the egg thing."

Bob smiled in satisfaction. He enjoyed knowing things you didn't. "Few people think about it. I have to go cross-country, just like in the old days. I'm right out there in wild country. Sometimes I find myself completely out of sight of any other person. I'll tell you, it gives you a different perspective. Why, I could take all my clothes off, and nobody would even know."

She just looked at him.

"Not that I've ever done that," he added quickly, "at least not fully."

Jamee wasn't sure she wanted to know more about this guy. "You walk?" she asked. "I've gone hiking in the Rockies and the Alps."

"No, of course not," Bob said with a wrinkled brow. "I couldn't carry all the equipment. I use an outdoor levitor."

She brightened. "I've seen you guys in those. They sort of look like a car. Pretty cozy, in fact."

"That's not the point," he said, waving off her remark irritably. "The point is, we're out there in the wild."

Where you could probably walk to the next working booth in a half-hour, she thought. "Just like the ol' Wild West," she quipped, affecting the twentieth-century accent.

He seemed oblivious to sarcasm. "Not nearly as dangerous," he confided seriously, "but I get a real feel for what it must have been like."

She couldn't keep herself from grinning at this.

He seemed to interpret her smile as adoration. "Out there," he announced grandly, waving his arm vaguely at the restaurant wall, "klicks from civilization, I can really understand the true grit that people were made of."

She propped her elbows on the table and cupped her chin in her palms. "Really?" she said, affecting a mirror of his own earnestness.

Bob nodded wisely. "Oh yes. It was survival of only the very fittest. We're just a bunch of coddled children by comparison."

She nodded her head within her palms. "Children," she repeated.

"We wouldn't have even measured up to their children. They had gun fights in school. We'd be cowering under the desks."

She remembered reading about that. Around the turn of the century, people would wake up one day and just snap—start shooting everybody they knew with machine guns. Even kids in high school would occasionally break into their father's arsenal. It culminated with the Goofy incident, where a Disney employee dressed in the floppy-eared outfit shot up the park, that finally convinced congress to convene a constitutional convention. The wording of the second amendment was changed to read, *In the absence of a local police force, citizens shall have the right to bear arms that cannot kill more than one person a second*, or something like that.

"I seem to remember that those kids were cowering under their desks," she observed.

Bob ignored this. "People worked eighty hours a week, and had to carry guns to protect themselves from drug dealers."

"Only because drugs were illegal then," she offered from her cradling palms.

He waved this off without comment. "And the police were no help. They were all corrupt and working for the mobs."

She had a vision of the village constable leading a pack of angry men, torches held high, as they climbed the hill to Dr. Frankenstein's castle. "I think you mean the Mob."

"What?" Bob said, seeming annoyed at the distraction.

"I think they referred to the Mafia as The Mob—singular."

"Of course," Bob said, scrunching his brow and giving his shoulders a quick shrug as though this was obvious. "People had to take the law into their own hands and go after the gangsters with a posse."

She raised an eyebrow. "Wasn't that the nineteenth century?"

"No," he said confidently, "they went after them in their cars."

She let it go. She wasn't confident enough to argue the point, and besides, there always seemed to be herds of cars chasing after each other in the movies of the time.

"Airplanes fell out of the sky," he went on. "It took courage to travel back then. Half the people that tried to fly the Wright Brother's planes died, you know, when they started to sell them."

Jamee closed one eye and peered at Bob out of the skeptical one. "The jets at the turn of the century were a far cry from the early Wright Brother's planes."

"Look it up if you don't believe me. Thousands and thousands of people died every year. It took a brave soul to get in one of those things and then climb ten klicks in the air, held up there by nothing but flimsy twentieth-century technology. The airlines wouldn't let the passengers bring parachutes along, you know. They were afraid that terrorists would bring a bomb on board, then jump out."

She lifted her head and sat back. Where the hell was the waiter? It was probably going to be a person, and how uncomfortable was *that* going to be?

"No argument from me," she assured. "I'd never get on one."

"It was the cars," he said.

Jamee sat looking at him from her slouched position, but he didn't elaborate. Would it be too rude to ignore his comment, maybe change the subject?

She sighed. "What was the cars, Bob?"

"That's where they got their character, their grit."

"Isn't grit dirt?"

He ignored her comment, apparently not concerned about being rude. "Once you left your driveway and headed out across the country, you were on your own. It was just you and your car. If something went wrong, if it broke down, you had to fix it or walk. Same as if a cowboy's horse got sick or died."

She was tempted to just agree with him. "They had tow trucks. They could call for help on their cell phones."

He smiled his patronizing smile. "Those came later, not until the twenties or thirties."

She knew he was wrong on that one; either that, or Sony Pictures had anticipated the cell phone by thirty years. She wasn't going to argue, though. She just wanted to get this over with.

"Do you know how a levitor works?" he asked, pointing to a waiter version gliding along with someone's meals.

She shrugged. "Only in a general way. It sort of shoots a kind of cloud of charged particles at the ground, then uses them to push against magnetically."

"Exactly," he said, surprising her with an apparent compliment. But when he continued, she realized that he meant his point, not her explanation. "We don't really know how things around us work. We're just a bunch of dumb passengers on this technology-driven earth—herded around by the scientists and engineers."

"Baa-aa," she said.

He blushed. She'd finally gotten through his sarcasm shield.

"My point," he said through tight lips, "is that people of the twentieth century had character because they were self-reliant.

They knew how the world they lived in worked." He glanced around the restaurant. "Where *is* the damn waiter, anyway?"

"Why do you wear those gloves?" she asked suddenly.

Her question surprised even her. Was she going on the offensive because she finally saw that she could get to him? If so, she assured herself, she was just defending herself against a supercilious bully.

Bob was staring at his covered hands. He looked up at her, and she saw resignation in his eyes. He knew he wasn't going to see her again after this dinner. He slowly pulled off his right glove and revealed a hairy hand, strong and muscular. Then, without looking at her again, he pulled off the left glove. Underneath, unbelievably, as though an overlaid hologram, was a woman's hand. There was no other way to think of it. The fingers were smooth and delicate, the wrist as thin as a tennis racket handle.

He looked up at her, and all she could do was shake her head in disbelief.

"A transporter accident," he said in a dull monotone. "I was trying out a new software release—an emergency feature that would generate a generic limb in the unlikely event that the transmission was disrupted. It hadn't been tested, but I figured it would work just fine. All that testing is just overkill anyway."

She looked at the woman's hand and back to his eyes. "Apparently not."

He sighed.

She nodded at the woman's hand. "That's the generic limb?"

She thought he wasn't going to answer at first, but he finally said, "No, it's an actual woman's hand."

Despite Jamee's resistance to it, the meaning of this sunk in. "There's a woman out there with your hand?" she asked in an excited whisper.

He nodded.

"My God!" she said out loud, putting her fingers to her mouth.

He nodded again. "I'm due in court next week."

"She's suing you," Jamee said, more a statement than a question. The poor woman wouldn't have the luxury of wearing gloves. Women don't wear gloves.

"She's suing Gee-TRIC, actually."

"I can't believe I haven't heard about this."

He shrugged.

"Of course!" she exclaimed, pretending to smack her forehead. "Gee-TRIC's covering it up."

Bob smiled sadly.

"I'm surprised they haven't fired you."

He pulled his left glove back over the feminine monstrosity. "They can't until after the trial."

She watched him until he lifted his eyes to her. "And then ...?"

He just returned her gaze grimly.

She didn't know what to say. He probably deserved what he was going to get. But it was an accident. The lunk was just an insecure boy who never grew up. But that poor woman ....

"Can I take your order?"

She jumped. A man in an archaic vest stood over her with a pad—a *paper* pad. What was she supposed to do now? Just tell him what she wanted, like in the old movies? She looked at Bob.

He smiled and nodded, and opened his menu. "I'll have the beef—that's real meat, right?"

ж ж ж

Jamee stood before the booth under the warm stars of San Diego. Bob had waved one last time before stepping in and disappearing. If she had lived at the turn of the century, she wouldn't even hesitate. She'd just walk right in and let her body be torn apart, atom-by-atom. She wouldn't even flinch. She'd have grit, real grit.

But she wasn't that person, and she couldn't fool herself. She couldn't drive a car, or fly an airplane, or shoot a gun at a drug dealer that was trying to rape her. Maybe Bob was right. Maybe people had lost their character when they started using the stupid booths.

How far was Boulder? Could she walk? No, it was on the other side of the Rockies. Wasn't it? She was never good at geography. Probably because she had no character.

She looked at her hands. She liked her hands. She didn't want to exchange them. She didn't want to get out of the booth "on the wrong foot."

What had Bob said? The booths were used a hundred million times a day. But he didn't actually say that they were used a hundred million times *flawlessly*.

She heard a man behind her clear his throat. Someone was waiting for the booth. She threw herself in and felt the freezing air of Boulder on her face. She put her hands to her face. They were her hands. She stepped out and walked to her apartment.

Who the hell needed character anyway?

Exposure

Guillermo wished that the Asian woman would find someone else to translate the coyote's commands. Actually, he wanted to wish this, he admitted to himself. He had been loyal to his wife for thirteen years, and he knew with certainty that he would continue to be. Five years working in the US while she stayed behind in Ensenada raising their three daughters—no, he reminded himself carefully, now just two—was test enough. If he'd had the capacity to cheat, he would have done so by now.

Still, this lithe woman with perfect, manzanita complexion tempted his attention. She hadn't demonstrated any interest herself beyond translation of the smuggler's instructions into English and he was glad for that.

At least, a part of him was glad.

He would be lying if he claimed that attraction to a beautiful woman was not deeply flattering. In Mexico, an engineer was respected and admired as an educated professional. He was on the threshold now of returning to a land where engineers were necessary to keep the gears of the world turning, but not invited to parties. Guillermo found it deeply ironic that he was forced to leave his home, where he was respected, to find lucrative work where he was tolerated with condescension.

"This is not your first time," the woman said as they lay in the stifling darkness of the abandoned tunnel waiting for word to continue.

Her accent was difficult to place, but her features were moderated Mongoloid, almost Caucasian. Guillermo wondered if one of her grandfathers was perhaps an American soldier sent to Vietnam to fight communists.

"This is my third opportunity to scurry like a rat across the border," he replied. "My work visa expired two years ago. Before that, I traveled like a human being."

"You went home to visit your family?"

The words for an answer formed in Guillermo's mind, but he only gasped, unable to breathe. He closed his eyes and clenched fingers, feeling them shake with the strain.

"I buried my daughter," he finally said.

"I . . . I'm sorry," the woman stuttered.

"So am I. She was my youngest. She went to the hospital with a broken leg, and died a few days later from infection."

"In . . . her leg?" the woman asked, incredulously.

"The IV drip. Apparently the needle was contaminated with MRSA germs."

"The fish that sank the boat," she observed.

"Excuse me?"

"A metaphor for resistant bacteria. A greedy fisherman takes so many fish, they finally cause his boat to sink."

Guillermo had assumed that the woman was an unskilled laborer like the rest of their dozen companions. Before he had a chance to ask about her background, though, rustling ahead was followed by word that they were moving again. He let the woman go ahead of him, and then he got up on his hands and knees and followed. Just like a dog, he thought. Or a rat.

The straw that the original drug smugglers had laid down years ago had deteriorated so that it disintegrated under their scampering into a fog of choking dry dust. Coughing slowed, but didn't stop, the incessant rambling jabber of the two college students behind him. The boys seemed excited and nervous, probably their first time across as fugitives. His eavesdropping revealed that they attended UCSD—or had. Perhaps, like himself, their visas had been terminated prematurely under the pressures of an American population floundering within a Service Economy that had, for decades, persevered stubbornly to sustain itself by selling imported goods to each other. Unlike the pretty Asian woman, they spoke fluent Spanish, but with an accent that tagged them as *Pocho*, a pejorative term for Mexican immigrants who have lived most of their lives in San Diego. If so, they should at least have green cards, and their presence in the tunnel was something of an enigma.

As Guillermo scurried forward fitfully, a bright glow ahead resolved into a small chamber large enough for half their group to stand up. He smelled the vague but oppressing odor of old, dried shit. He wondered if one of his companions hadn't perhaps manifested his fright with excremental abandon.

There was barely room for Guillermo to climb to his feet behind the Asian woman, but the two students pushed on through and stood up, leaving hardly room for the rest to even breathe.

The coyote, a small, perpetually angry man, had climbed part way up a crude ladder along one side and rasped a hoarse, whispered command for the rest to stay in the tunnel for the moment. Then, with a disapproving shake of his head at his incompetent charges, he climbed to the top, lifted an oval hatch, and peered out into blinding California daylight. Guillermo could see the butt of the handgun sticking out from under his belt. When he'd asked the guide about it earlier, the gruff reply had been, "For rattlesnakes."

"We're lucky that it's daytime," one of the students with an unruly mop of braided hair gushed.

His friend, wearing a T-shirt scrawled across the front with *Immunize Against Authority* replied, "I made sure before I signed us up."

From behind Guillermo, the Asian woman added, "The crossings are always during the day."

All the people in the chamber were squeezed together like commuters in a Japanese Bullet Train, and Guillermo could feel the woman's breasts pressed firmly against his back. He knew she couldn't help it, and he tried his best to ignore the sensual contact.

"Good for us," Mop-hair affirmed, "but for ten thousand dollars, you'd expect a minimum of competence from a coyote."

Ten thousand dollars was the standard fare charged by the California coyote cartel.

"What do you mean?" the Asian woman asked.

"Ospreys," Mop-hair replied. "The coyote is leading everybody right to them."

Osprey were miniaturized military surveillance drones that the Border Patrol had recently put into service, and Mop-hair didn't seem overly concerned at the prospect of encountering one.

"Actually," Guillermo cut in, "the coyote knows exactly what he's doing. At night we would blaze away in infrared like human flares."

Actually, he corrected himself silently, dusk was the ideal time as daylight failed but the ground was still warm. Their schedule, however, was dictated by the cartel-arranged ride waiting beyond a low ridge.

"But at least at night, crossers would be caught by patrolmen," T-shirt Boy offered.

"Isn't that exactly what we want to avoid?" the Asian woman asked.

"I mean, rather than stung by a drone."

"You believe that stuff?" the woman challenged.

"It's all over the web—personal accounts."

To Guillermo, *all over the web* usually meant a story, whatever its veracity, which was simply sensational or scandalous enough to pass along. "I've read that some Osprey have the ability to anesthetize a target, but they would be used only in extreme situations, where someone was in danger, for example."

"Who says?" demanded Mop-hair.

"That's the kind of propaganda they want you to believe," T-shirt Boy growled.

"How *do* you know this?" the Asian woman asked Guillermo quietly into his ear.

He wished he could see her face.

He shrugged, jostling other shoulders. "From engineering periodicals."

He didn't mention that he had colleagues that worked on the video downlinks of some of the larger drones. In fact, he scolded himself, he should have kept his mouth shut altogether. Once you cross the border, the boundaries of your life should collapse inside you.

"Like they're going to tell you the truth," T-shirt Boy scoffed.

Guillermo said nothing. Keep your life inside your own skin.

After a few moments, though, he couldn't resist. "So, what's your source of truth?"

"Anybody not under Big Brother's control."

"Which presumably eliminates pretty much everybody in America," Guillermo concluded, meaning to be facetious.

T-shirt Boy missed the sarcasm. "Exactly. You have to look to foreign sources."

The radical young men's perspective seemed to come from inside the USA, as though members of that society, deepening the mystery of their inclusion in the sardine crush waiting to burst through to the Land of Opportunity.

"Like Al Jazeera," Guillermo suggested.

He wasn't being sarcastic now. The Arabic news media was one he often consulted.

"Yeah, or Xinhua."

"Oh really?" Guillermo exclaimed, surprised.

These boys were indeed either radical or just stupid. Accessing the Chinese news was the quickest way to swing the NSA's gaze towards you, even more so than Al Jazeera. This was no blown-up internet hoax-turned-urban myth. Ever since China lost all its billions of American investment in the greatest international foreclosure in history, neither side had a vested interest any longer in hiding the fact that they were still cold war adversaries. Now, though, market evaluations replaced ICBMs as weapon delivery systems.

"Yeah, really," T-shirt Boy shot back. "Not everybody's cowed into submission, you know."

Guillermo wasn't sure why he wanted to goad the young man. Maybe he was just jealous that they could still afford to take risks.

"There's lots of ways of getting to the Chinese sites without being traced. You're smart boys, you should be able to figure it out."

He had.

"I don't think we should—" the Asian woman started to say, but T-shirt Boy cut her off.

"We don't just read Xinhua, we *talk* to them."

Guillermo heard the Asian woman suck her teeth in disapproval.

"You post comments," Guillermo derided. "Oh boy! Now that's what I call turning the cattle prod around."

T-shirt Boy just snorted. Guillermo had expected a violent reaction to his ridicule, but he realized that college students spend their days parrying insults.

"We don't just post comments," Mop-hair joined in. "We work with them."

"We're not supposed to say anything," T-shirt Boy chastised in a whisper, as though Guillermo couldn't hear from six inches away.

"We're almost there," Mop-hair defended. "What difference does it make now?" To Guillermo, he added, "We're with the *Guardian*, the UCSD newspaper."

"You're . . . on assignment?"

That would explain US citizens crawling through an abandoned drug smuggling tunnel thirty miles from San Diego.

"We're here to reveal the underhanded methods of the Border Patrol."

Guillermo had the idea that reporters were supposed to first investigate issues and gather information, and that revelations then followed as the result of unbiased analysis.

He addressed instead what most concerned him, though. "But, you're also working with Xinhua?"

"I think that this is really enough," the Asian woman demanded.

Her passion surprised Guillermo.

Before the student reporters were able to spill more beans, though, the coyote barked down from above that it was time to go.

Ж Ж Ж

Guillermo waited inside the old outhouse for the command to come out. The coyote squatted in the dirt just outside the creaky door watching the second of his charge sprint across the open ground to a cluster of brush-infested boulders a hundred yards away.

The original drug smugglers were nothing if not wily. When the border fence came through decades before, the owners of this dirt-scrabble ranch took the buyout money and made for an easier life, leaving the squat plank buildings to bleach in the desert sun. The tunnel builders had masterfully come up directly under the outhouse and hauled away years of accumulated crap back into Mexico. Voila, a state-side exit station. This explained the shit Guillermo had smelled, and the oval hatch he'd seen from below.

Apparently satisfied with the result of the first couple of guinea pigs, the coyote began frantically waving them all through the doorway. Guillermo, the Asian woman, and two other women he hadn't talked to were ready to make a dash for safety. The two students along with all the rest would have to crawl up through the toilet seat one by one as room became available in the small shithouse. Guillermo hesitated, unsure about the protocol here: normally a gentleman would let a woman go first, but what if there was the potential for danger?

The two other women didn't wait for him to figure it out. They burst through the doorway and ran for the boulders as fast as their short legs could carry them. Tote bags and plastic milk jugs of water swayed and banged so that it looked to be a struggle just to stay upright. With a quick nod for good luck, the Asian woman took off after them, and Guillermo followed as the shaggy black mass of Mop-hair appeared inside the toilet seat, looking disconcertedly like the head of John the Baptist served up for Herod.

Halfway to the safety of the boulders, Guillermo stopped and froze. He heard an engine, the distinctive burring whine of a prop. He quickly scanned the faultless blue expanse of sky as he debated whether to return to the outhouse, but found not even a bird. A young man, bowed under the weight of a clean, new backpack, pushed past him, nearly knocking him over. Mop-hair and T-shirt Boy held back as well, standing off to the side of the camouflaged port of entry terminal and peering around as though expecting the airplane to appear out of thin air next to them.

The sound of the engine and propeller diminished and faded into the distance, and Guillermo started again for the boulders as his racing heart eased the struggle to pound its way out from his chest.

He made it to the boulders where the Asian woman stood next to the others, who were crouched together in an apprehensive flock, but he turned when he heard an excited shout from behind. Mop-hair was pointing emphatically, and T-shirt Boy peered along the gestured direction, trying to see as well.

Guillermo saw. A humming bird hovered and flitted about the head of the next crosser, an older man carrying a battered little suitcase that he swung about ineffectually at his harasser.

Guillermo knew that this was no humming bird, though. He'd never seen one, but he immediately recognized it as an Osprey, and he marveled at the miracle of miniaturized electronics and nano-machine technology of the surveillance vehicle. It seemed quaintly anachronistic to even think of it as a "vehicle." Somewhere, miles away, a human monitored and directed the device, but the role was more of a flight controller or squadron commander than pilot. The tiny drone had a brain that knew how to fly and maneuver, and only required tactical direction for its mission.

Suddenly, as though one of those mission commands had been received loud and clear, the flitting drone paused a foot above the hapless man. An instant later it jerked back in recoil as what appeared to be a spider thread, glinting a moment in the sun, bridged the gap between its nose and the man's chest. For that instant, burned in Guillermo's brain in stop-action film, the drone's eyes—black, depthless glass lens flush with the body—stared on in malevolent disregard, devoid of emotion or the capacity to be swayed from its directive.

The man stared down at his chest, dropped the suitcase, and placed both his hands over the spot where the tiny needle had struck, appearing to ready himself for benediction. The effect was eerily enhanced when he dropped to his knees, where he swayed a moment before falling senseless under the effects of the powerful anesthesia.

"Who was in danger there?" the Asian woman whispered next to him.

He looked at her in shock and puzzlement.

"So much for using the knockout punch only in extreme situations," she quipped sardonically, quoting him.

The woman's demeanor had changed. Where before, gathering at the border and then in the tunnel, she had been just another member of the flock, her body language now spoke of confidence, as though she could manage just fine from here without the coyote.

Guillermo shook his head in consternation. He didn't answer, for mayhem was breaking out before them. There were now two Osprey drones zipping about like wasps protecting their nest. Another crosser was down, a teenage boy, crumpled in the dirt. Amazingly, Mop-hair had run out into the expanse between the outhouse and the boulder, shouting and waving his arms. One of the drones twisted, rose, and then dove straight for the student. Incredibly, the boy stood his ground, arms outstretched as though daring the miniature fighter-bomber to try to take him. The drone stopped just beyond arm's reach, its soulless lens eyes studying him.

Guillermo watched as the second drone circled around behind Mop-hair. He wanted to shout warning, but the woman gripped his arm in restraint, as though reading his mind. Surely the boy must know what was happening. The second drone eased up, a foot above the shaggy mop of hair. The boy's shoulders hunched slightly. *Son of a bitch*, Guillermo thought, *he wants to be stung!* The infinitely thin spider web flashed, and Mop-hair involuntarily slapped the back of his neck. He spun around, but the attacking Osprey had already backed away and flown off for the next target. The boy sat down to wait, and seconds later keeled over, looking all the world as though an off-scene movie director had shouted the order.

Guillermo saw T-shirt Boy standing in the shade of the outhouse holding his cell phone, catching the action.

Again, he heard a buzzing whine, and the Asian woman was shoving something into his hands. It was a rain poncho. "Cover yourself," she explained as she squatted and pulled her own over her.

He caught a blur of motion against the blue sky as he imitated her, while the rest of their little huddled flock broke screaming and running.

He adjusted the poncho and could feel that it was of high quality—tightly woven fabric, with a soft, inner chaff layer. He wondered if the drone's needles could penetrate a cheap plastic raincoat.

The shouts and pounding feet just beyond his protective shield diminished, but, ominously, not with distance, but through thinning. Finally, the last pleading babble morphed into a moan, a thud, and then there was silence.

Not quite total silence, though. The buzz of angry wasps moved up and around, and then closed in. Guillermo made himself small, shivering as he waited for the flagitious prick against his back.

A glimpse of movement caused him to snap his head to the side. His motion moved the poncho, and one of the drones eased sideways, positioning itself again in the opening through which his head would normally protrude. For one second, Guillermo stared into the blank, polished eyes of evil intent before he jerked the poncho and wrapped the opening in his fist, closing it.

The insistent buzzing swung this way and that around Guillermo, and he thought the tension would force him to fling off the coat and run for it, but shouting finally drew the little devil away.

Guillermo remained huddled under his poncho shield, shivering in the oven heat as the noon sun baked the dark cloth. He heard rustling—the Asian Woman was casting off her poncho and getting up. Reasoning that she wouldn't be standing there if the drones were still nearby, he slowly pulled away the cloth and stood up. The senseless bodies of his fellow crossers lay motionless all around him. They looked dead, but he assured himself that this was just a testament to the effectiveness of the anesthesia. Somewhere, off in the distance, he was aware of the ubiquitous hum of the airplane.

Another shout drew his attention back to the outhouse. T-shirt Boy stood waving his arms in wide sweeps at the crumpled heap of Mop-hair. He seemed angry, as though trying to wake his friend. Then Guillermo noticed an Osprey drone hovering above the fallen student, facing the angry boy with calm disregard.

The hum of the approaching airplane swelled to a menacing minor roar.

The sound of the airplane engine and propeller was modulated with a higher-pitched buzz, though. Guillermo realized that this second component sound was close by, off to the side.

He spun to find the second Osprey watching them from five feet away. Instinctively, he raised his arms in defense, but the drone made no move.

Guillermo lowered his arms. "Why don't they attack?" he asked wonderingly.

"Out of needles," the Asian woman replied, rooting around in her bag.

Of course, Guillermo thought. There were at least ten unconscious bodies.

The woman found what she was looking for: a compact, high-end video camera, essentially an ovoid just large enough to hold a set of lenses. Strapped to it with tie-wraps was a slim box, what he took to be external storage.

An explosion caused him to flinch and cower.

It was a gunshot. T-shirt Boy was holding the coyote's handgun in both fists, swinging it in wide arcs as he tried to follow the evading drone. Guillermo hadn't seen the coyote among the fallen. Their shepherd had probably beaten a scrambled retreat back through the tunnel.

He glanced at the woman. She was intent, watching a bright, tiny screen on the camera. She was filming T-shirt Boy's tirade at being excluded from among the anesthetized chosen. On the side of the strapped-on box, red and green LEDs blinked out a dance of unrecognizable rhythm. Somehow the mix of red and green seemed to Guillermo's engineering mind as incongruous, but that mind had no spare MIPs to deal with it.

The roar of the approaching airplane expanded to a screaming crescendo. The enraged student didn't seem to notice. The second drone had joined the dance as they both looped in dizzying arcs—electrons sweeping urgent orbits around the dense, immobile nucleus that was the boy. The intention was clearly to keep their armed target occupied until the plane arrived.

And it finally arrived at that moment.

From the scale of the machine's roar among the expanse of the silent desert, Guillermo was expecting perhaps a Harrier, but the unmanned vehicle that emerged through the watery heat waves struck him as ludicrously small. Barely a hundred feet above the sand, the attack drone rushed forward, hauled along by toy-like turboprops, one mounted on each wing. Gaping from its belly, lending the appearance of a small shark charging for the killing bite, a weapons bay sheltered protruding snouts of gun barrels.

As the condor-sized mother ship approached, the dragonfly drones pulled up and away, and T-shirt Boy was left to face the newcomer. The propeller casings rotated skywards as the attack drone settled in, converting the small-scale plane into a dual-prop helicopter, so that the slack-jawed mechanical shark came to a halt twenty feet from the raging student and the same distance above.

The boy turned to face the roaring beast, blinking and turning his face from the howling storm of dust blasting past him. He held the gun in clenched fists before him at the end of stiff arms.

Guillermo read the body language revealed in the knotted biceps, and the meaning played out terrifyingly in his mind.

"No!" he shouted. "Don't—"

The Asian woman had reached out one arm to silence him, even as she continued to film the event.

It hardly mattered, since his voice was lost in the shriek of the artificial tornado.

And, in any case, it was too late, for, as though accepting a fate beyond his control, T-shirt Boy lifted his arms and yanked the trigger. His locked elbows carried the recoil to his shoulders and jerked his whole body backwards.

The bullet missed the target, and the hovering menace proffered no chance for a second try. Before the boy could recover, bursts of liquid white light flashed from the shark's teeth as it spat its own lethal response.

T-shirt Boy seemed to explode. The barrage of drone bullets tore through his body so thoroughly that it looked like his blood had burst through a dam to spray forth under tremendous pressure.

The attack drone recovered from its own recoil as though bobbing from a passing wave. It just hovered there above the ruined mass of torn flesh and blood that had been, seconds ago, an angry student.

"Run for it," the Asian woman urged beside Guillermo.

Exposure

His head was a beehive of frantic, siren thoughts bouncing and ricocheting off the sides of his skull. Running away was indeed what his gut pleaded to do, and he even turned and started off, but he dove to the ground instead and scrambled behind a bush.

Maybe it was an ancient instinct, not invoked for centuries, that running from a predator defined you as prey. Maybe it was just the subconscious part of his brain that assimilated and correlated information.

He wanted to go home, home to his wife and two remaining daughters—home, where he could speak his native language and let down his guard about appearing sufficiently American.

But the attack drone had moved over to the outhouse where the two Osprey tenders flitted about, in and out of the doorway.

The Asian woman continued to film it all, reeling off a continuous, quiet commentary in her own singsong tongue.

Suddenly Guillermo felt an overpowering urge to get away from her—not to run, though, as she had suggested. His subconscious was finally reaching conclusions.

He clawed sideways to better cover behind a rock. There was something in her running commentary . . . despite the inhuman horror, her words flowed in polished narrative style. Even in her foreign Asian tongue, this was obvious. Her whole demeanor, in fact, was purposeful, almost business-like.

A concussion slammed his face as the outhouse inflated into a roiling ball of orange and black destruction. Taken by surprise, the woman babbled a moment reflexively, but quickly recovered and resumed her measured story.

It was like the final piece of puzzle slipping into place. Guillermo realized that the spontaneous words spoken in shocked distraction were not the same language of the commentary. For a brief, involuntary moment, the woman had relaxed back to her own native tongue.

"You're with Xinhua!" he hissed.

She glanced at him, held his gaze a moment, and then returned to her task without comment.

It was true.

He turned the focus knob in his head and the picture of the last ten minutes resolved into sharp focus. Like the naive students, she too was on assignment. What was the chance of two news organizations picking the same crossing group?

Indeed.

She'd been ready for the student's escapade, expecting it. In fact, she'd probably had an invisible hand in manipulating the situation, maneuvering the boys into an idealistic grab at exposing tiny anesthetizing drones, unaware that they were pawns in a larger unmasking—one infinitely more brutal, and commensurately valuable to an adversary.

Mop-hair and T-shirt Boy had bragged that they worked with the Xinhua. They had no clue that one of the news agency's reporters had been standing right next to them.

And, it wouldn't do to send a Chinese national; that would have been too obvious.

Her bag lay on its side on the ground, and he saw that a small handgun had rolled out. Guillermo guessed that, had T-shirt Boy not picked up the coyote's, this one would have found its way to him.

Echoes of the outhouse obliteration melted away among the surrounding hills, leaving just the numbing background roar of the attack drone.

"You picked a large crossing group on purpose," he said quietly.

She glanced again quickly at him, with irritation now, but, again, made no comment, simply returning to her task of filming.

"You had to make sure the Osprey drones would run out of needles."

She was angry now as she turned and jabbed an extended forefinger flat against her pressed lips.

"Am I ruining the story?" he taunted.

His own anger was starting to boil. How could he view her as anything but a murderer? He realized that she had probably tried to get him to run on the chance that she might film a second attack drone execution.

She turned completely around now, and menace filled her eyes. Holding the camera in one hand, she reached down, picked up the handgun, and pointed it at him.

Guillermo froze, his mind racing. Would she dare shoot and draw attention? Should he take a chance and try to duck down behind the rock? His perceptions seemed to extend and expand, as though his mind had shifted into a new gear that allowed him to process many inputs at once. Curiously, it was the blinking red and green LEDs that caught his attention. They danced and flickered, almost purposefully mimicking the chaos and danger surrounding them. In fact, that's what a blinking red LED implied, a visible indication that something was wrong.

There, in the expanded state of consciousness suspended at the tip of a loaded handgun, Guillermo suddenly understood that the little box strapped to the camera was not external storage. That was silly. The camera, no matter how small, would host the capacity for hours of record time on its own.

No, the box was something else—an uplink. Xinhua was hedging its bet that their agent would escape safely with the footage. The box was simultaneously transmitting the video to a Chinese satellite.

Or trying to.

The link was obviously marginal. The red LED meant the link was broken. It flickered and blinked as the connection came and went. The resulting video would be garbled, hardly recognizable.

He wanted to explain this to her. He was an engineer, after all. But she was pointing a gun at him.

He didn't have to decide. The screaming roar of the twin turbo props moved and swelled, and the monstrously evil face of the attack drone suddenly loomed above her.

The Xinhua reporter spun and fell back with a cry, tripping and falling. As Guillermo peeked around from behind his rock, the hovering menace settled closer, as though getting a better look at its victim.

The woman, her hair whipping in the prop's blast, regained her composure somewhat and sat up. She lifted the camera so that the two mechanical imaging devices stared unblinking at each other. Then, slowly, she lifted her free hand, extending the middle finger in universal defiance.

The controller of the attack drone may have simply wavered a moment, fingers cramped and tired from holding a joystick in precise positions. Or, being human, the man may have met the woman's challenge with a gesture of his own. Whatever the reason, the flying arsenal sank slightly towards the defiant reporter, and she leaned back, retracting the provocative finger to brace her hand on the ground behind her.

The fearless and competent woman, the covert news media agent who had orchestrated the story of the week that would measurably weaken America's public world face, didn't notice that her hand was about to land on the gun she had dropped.

The attack drone operator did, though.

For a second time, fire erupted from the shark teeth and blood sprayed into the air. Something else shot upward as well. A reflex spasm as the bullets tore through the woman flung the expensive camera skyward. It was just a fleeting blur of motion, but it blossomed into dozens of scattering offspring as it met the mincing prop blades. Pieces of plastic pattered down like rain all around Guillermo.

The dying flinch of the Xinhua reporter produced one last consequence, which probably saved Guillermo's life. The expensive camera, although insignificant when dashed against a Harrier jet, was wholly significant when contacting the attack drone's ten-inch propeller at six thousand RPMs. With sufficient altitude, the operator might have recovered and limped back to base. He had chosen, though, to intimidate the woman. As the shattered pieces of camera rained on Guillermo, the attack drone listed hard to starboard and spun sharply clockwise. The operator, perhaps panicking as he desperately tried to recover, overcompensated, and the heavy machine nosed into the dying woman. A sickening thump, like a butcher knife slammed into a ripe watermelon, was immediately followed by squealing shrieks of tearing metal as the killing drone crashed into the boulders. The grinding annihilation seemed to go on forever as Guillermo cowered behind his rock before either the gas tank or ordinance ignited and jolted his bones with the shock of a deafening explosion.

And then there was silence, except for fading echoes and tinkling of metal falling about to join the remnants of the wholly significant camera.

Guillermo lay curled behind his rock gasping for breath. He had a difficult time grasping what had transpired over the last few minutes. T-shirt Boy was dead. The Asian woman was dead, horribly mangled. The attack drone, the versatile predatory flying machine that surely would have eliminated him as a witness, was destroyed.

His ears clanged with his own inner echoes of the explosion, but through the ringing buzz, he could discern the same distant industrious whir they'd heard before: the vanquished attack drone's brother was on the way.

And the two tiny Ospreys were somewhere nearby.

Perhaps they'd been destroyed along with their mother ship.

Or, perhaps not.

If they found him, he was a dead man for sure. They would track him until the second attack drone arrived. He forced himself to unwrap and look around. The dragonfly drones were nowhere in sight. If they had survived the attack drone's violent end, they would surely come soon to investigate the aftermath.

What was left of the Asian woman was pure nightmare. The explosion had thrown her body against a boulder outcrop nearly tearing her in two. Guillermo gagged and fell onto his hands and knees to keep from fainting.

The Ospreys would be here soon.

There was only one way out, and he wasn't sure he could carry it through. He had no choice but to try. Retching and shivering in turn, he knelt next to the mangled woman's body and slid his fingers across the exposed still-warm torn flesh, and then, groaning with effort, smeared them across his chin, nose, and forehead. Growling like an animal, hysterical with disgust and pity, he grabbed the two sides of his shirt and yanked so that buttons popped and flew away in desperate escape. He coated his palms with the woman's blood and painted his chest, and then, nearly insane with the horror he was committing, he massaged the gruesome blood into his hair and slid his hands down the sides of his head across his ears and cheeks.

He was done. Whether it was sufficient or not, he was done. Any more wasn't worth living for.

Still on hands and knees, he crawled ten feet away and propped himself against a rock. Changing his mind, he lay in the dirt on his side, splaying his arms and legs in what he imagined might be random positions.

And then he closed his eyes and tried to look dead. It was an easy task; it was simply method acting.

Through the inner ringing, which he wasn't sure would ever go away, Guillermo heard excited buzzing. Flies seemed to exude from the very rocks of the desert. The burr of the voracious insects wove together in a complex pattern as they circled him like an array of satellites. One after another, they alighted on his arms and chest, nearly driving him mad as they crawled about harvesting their morbid meal.

When they found his face to crawl about his cheeks, scale his nose, and even tread his eyelids, the urge to twitch and swipe them away was overwhelming, and was only prevented by a larger buzzing that swelled in dominance as it arrived. Fleeing what they must have taken for their own great predator, the flies scattered, replaced by a gentle breeze that was both refreshing and ominous.

Guillermo held his breath and willed every cell of his body to be still.

The whirring of artificial gossamer wings and wash of air across his face held steady, as though the Osprey was studying him. Guillermo imagined that if he were to open his eyes, he would be staring into another pair that was black and inanimate, not unlike those of the flies it replaced.

He could hold his breath and keep his mind contained inside the shell he willed into hibernation only so long. In the end, his own countrymen saved him. The demolition of the outhouse and the attack drone's demise had attracted two ranchers to the other side of the fence. Guillermo could hear them debating the meaning of the hole where the ancient plank shelter had been. One man thought that it might have been caused by a buildup of methane from the stored contents, but the other confided that he knew of the tunnel, and that he feared that there was now hell to be paid.

Whether or not the Osprey operator understood the words, he must have decided that these Mexicans needed investigating, for the gentle wash of air disappeared, and the gossamer whirring lifted up and away.

Guillermo waited ten, twenty seconds more, but finally had to suck in a lung full of air. He opened his eyes and turned his head, but there were no Ospreys, only the returning flies.

He pushed himself up and got to his feet. He avoided looking in the direction of the woman, and, keeping his eyes to the ground, he started off through the jumble of boulders, into the heartland of the country where so much destruction had come down.

He wished with all his heart that he could scale the fence and return home, but the second attack drone was drawing ever closer.

Something caught his eye. It was just one piece among a sea of blasted debris, but it piqued the engineer. He picked it up. It was a tiny circuit board, a typical example of miniaturized electronics. At first he thought it might have come from the attack drone, but a remnant of gray plastic casing still clung to a jack wire, and he realized that he was holding the heart of the woman's camera.

Added to the horror of the deaths was the tragedy of the futility. The woman had carefully orchestrated it all, only to be unknowingly foiled by an intermittent satellite link. Blinking red LEDs were the bane of mankind.

He was about to toss the circuit board aside as scrap, but something, some wisp of notion, whispered in his head. Maybe it followed from admiration that the more dense his colleagues shrank circuitry, the more durable the result. He stood staring at the camera remnant as a new attack drone approached and two Ospreys flitted about nearby and marveled that unlike the woman's memories that melted within minutes of her death, non-volatile silicon memory lasted virtually forever.

And here it was.

The satellite link had been backup, insurance against just the sort of thing that had transpired. The camera, though, would have simultaneously stored the video. The billions of bits of image information—the indiscriminate anesthetization of crossers, the murder of T-shirt Boy, the final confrontation—were all there, waiting to be retrieved and reconstructed.

Guillermo slipped the circuit board into his pocket and smiled wanly. He could be the backup to the backup; he could deliver the footage to Xinhua. Indeed, he might even be able to arrange a price—a reward. Regardless, though, the Americans had to be exposed.

He started off at a trot, keeping to the boulders and occasional bushes where available.

He stopped.

Something wasn't right.

He looked back, but the mangled body of the Asian woman was already out of view.

What was it?

He knew. It wasn't the woman, but the boy. T-shirt Boy had lost his life, trampled unheeded underfoot as two mighty nations wrestled for economic position.

He took the circuit board from his pocket and clenched his fingers around it. Delivering the footage to Xinhua was tantamount to condoning the boy's manipulation, was joining into the unholy scheme.

He considered stomping it underfoot, but slipped it back into his pocket and ran off. No sense throwing the baby out with the bath water. He'd find a use. Maybe he would mail it to the *Guardian* at UCSD.

Hell, maybe he'd send the blood-won package to Al Jazeera.

The sound of the second attack drone grew louder, and Guillermo ran for his life through the southern California desert. He ran away from the mechanized drones of the American Border Patrol, but he also ran towards their disclosure.

The Devil You Say

The only ghosts Chuck had ever seen came knocking just once a year, and, at three feet and dribbling snot, lacked ghoulish menace. Additionally, sinister effect was diluted by a mother holding a hand, since the holes were never positioned where the ghost was actually looking. Said mother invariably seemed embarrassed that she was too busy for something more intriguing than a ruined sheet.

Consequently, two aspects about this particular ghost appearing before him were startling: one was that this specimen was not too busy to outfit himself in vest, top-hat, and coat with tails, and the other was that it was not Halloween.

Actually, there was a third aspect as well, and this was the one that jolted Chuck into tossing his book and scrambling from his chair, nearly falling down in the process—Chuck hadn't answered the door to let him in.

"What the hell . . ." Chuck stammered, balanced between fear and anger.

"Indeed," the ghost agreed in the precise British accent of Jeremy Brett's Sherlock Holmes. "My sentiments exactly."

In fact, based on rambunctious sideburns and attentive, if slightly puzzled, countenance, the ghost could have been instead Dr. Watson, albeit on his way to a Victorian wedding.

That the intruder comprised a ghost was implied by the table lamp visible through his waistcoat and the soles of his patent leather shoes disassociated from the carpet by a few inches.

"Very sorry to bother you, chap," the Watson wraith went on, wringing his hands nervously, "but I seem to have gotten myself into a bit of a pinch."

Chuck shook his head slowly, not sure what to say.

"I'd be ever so thankful if you could help," Watson implored, holding his hand out to his sides, where the tips of the fingers faded as though airbrushed away.

"Who . . . *what* the hell are you?" Chuck finally managed.

Watson sighed. "I was afraid that would come up."

"Well, yea-ah!"

The wraith stared at him curiously, then wagged his head in consternation. "Let me inquire of you: do I appear . . . odd to you?"

"You mean besides the fact that you are a ghost?"

"A ghost? Oh, dear no—not a ghost. But, besides that part."

"How about the fact that your clothes are about a century out of date?"

"Ah!" Watson exclaimed, snapping his fingers soundlessly. "I suppose that would explain things."

"Er, it was me looking for explanations, remember?"

Watson seemed lost in thought. "I, you mean."

"What?"

The non-ghost looked up at him. "I believe you meant to say, 'It was I that was looking for explanations.' And, unfortunately, I'm afraid time is pressing sufficiently to prevent me fabricating a likely story, and, therefore, I shall have to tell you the truth. I am not of your species, not of this planet."

"To hell, you say!"

"Hmm, I'm not sure I follow that expression, but the concept of hell does seem to be at the root of my current problem. So, it seems that you could indeed be of aid to me."

Watson turned towards the door and gestured for him to follow.

"Not so fast! Are you telling me that you're an alien?"

"An alien," Watson repeated as though tasting the word in his mouth. "If an alien is someone who is not a citizen of this country, then, in that sense, yes, I guess I am an alien."

"I meant a space alien."

"Space-alien—interesting juxtaposition of words."

"You really are from, like, 1890, aren't you?"

"What year is it now?"

"2010."

"Oh dear!" Watson cried, putting his hand to his mouth. "Vragbushlingtit really slipped one over on me!"

"Are you a time traveler?"

"Hmm, no," the ghostly-man murmured distractedly. "No such thing as traveling through time."

"Then what in God's name *are* you?"

Watson looked up sharply. "God indeed—you really are the man to help me. Let's go."

Chuck watched as the nattily-dressed man walked through the closed door. A few seconds later his head popped back through. "Aren't you coming?"

"Not until I get those answers."

Watson emerged back through the door nodding resignedly. "Let's keep it to the minimum, though, shall we? This is becoming quite painful."

"Well, ex-cu-uuse me! I'm not the one who came waltzing uninvited into my apartment!"

The incorporeal man stared at him confused a moment before understanding brightened his face. "No, I don't mean that our conversation is painful—I was referring to . . . my problem."

"Okay. Short and sweet. Where are you from?"

"Er, I don't know how to explain. I lack the English word for my sun. If we step outside, I might be able to point it out to you. On the other hand, I'm not sure we could see it from here. In fact, come to think of it, I doubt I could actually decipher its location from here."

"Never mind. The point is, you're from another star."

"Oh yes! I thought that we cleared that up when we determined that I am a space alien."

"Fine. Now we're getting somewhere. How did you get here?"

"How did I get here? Why, that's an odd question . . . ah, right. I keep forgetting the consequences of your planet being quarantined."

"Huh? We're, like, contagious?"

"No, no. Culturally quarantined. You're whole planet is kept isolated to preserve the primitive quality."

"Ha! No kidding? The UFO nuts were right all along—there really is a Prime Directive."

"Excuse me?"

"Prime Directive—just what you're talking about. Direct contact with a new civilization has to be limited and hidden."

"Actually, contact with new civilizations is fine."

"But you said that Earth is under quarantine . . . wait a second! You're saying that we're not *civilized*?"

Watson held out his hands in supplication. "It's all relative, what?"

"What, indeed . . . hey, so, why are *you* here?"

"Right," Watson agreed, "we come to the rub. You see, I'm not supposed to be here."

"Like, you're supposed to be somewhere else? Nineteenth century England, perhaps?"

"No, like not on the planet at all. I explained; it's quarantined. Only a very few permits are granted at any time, and they're almost exclusively issued to anthropologists."

"Which, I take it, you're not?"

"Dear no! Goodness no! I'm a . . . what you might call a thespian."

"You're an actor?"

"An actor, yes. I've come to study for a part."

"What! Let me get this straight: you're an alien actor who's sneaked onto Earth to study playing us in some sort of space movie?"

"Movie?"

"Recorded theatre."

"Ah, exactly right. I deduce that direct exposure will give me a leg-up in the auditions."

"You don't even have the part yet?"

"It seems a shoe-in."

"Right. On the other hand, you're not fitting in very well right now."

Watson stood erect and lifted his nose. "*That* is not my fault."

"Let me guess: you're going to blame it on Vragabullshit, or whatever his name is."

"Vragbushlingtit. And most definitely. He's obviously playing a prank on me. It is not conceivable that he allocated an aura and language score one hundred years out of date by mistake. I should have seen this coming. That man could hold a grudge until the galaxies collide."

"Aura?"

Watson glided his hands down his front, showing off his digs. "What you see. A visual projection."

"You're not even here—on the planet?"

"Oh, I am here all right. But not in this room."

"Where, then?"

"I'm out on the sidewalk."

"So . . . why don't you come in—you know, yourself?"

"I can't. That is the problem. That is why I came to you for help, many minutes ago, I might add."

"I don't understand. What kind of trouble? Why can't you come in?"

"There are three men sitting on me."

"What!" Chuck exclaimed, heading for the door. "Why didn't you tell me?"

"I have been trying. Believe me, I have."

Chuck hurried down the hall as the alien's visual projection appeared through the wall and fell in next to him, stepping along six inches above the floor.

They passed door after door of Chuck's neighbors. "Why did you pick me?"

"I tapped into your planet's communications network and discovered that you are a naturalist. I surmised that a man of science would be a likely candidate to understand my situation."

"I'm not that kind of naturalist—I sell organic sugar."

Watson just stared at him.

"There's all kinds of pesticides in normal sugar," Chuck offered.

"Ah, that explains it, then."

"That explains what?"

"Er, let's just say it explains a representative median cognitive position in a primitive society structure."

Chuck stopped, and a second later the projection of Watson was suddenly facing him without actually turning around.

"Please don't be offended," the projection pleaded. "Like I said before, I don't have time to fabricate untruths."

"Well, just remember," Chuck muttered continuing on, "it's you who came to me for help."

They crossed the shabby lobby, and Watson's aura slipped silently through the front door. Chuck followed, using the primitive median cognitive method of opening the door. He stepped out onto the stoop, and Watson stood there pointing down. Three men were indeed sitting on him—the real him—off to the side, near the wall of the apartment building. The real Watson flickered and wavered under the three rear ends. Chuck saw that the flickering was just instability of that Victorian-clad aura, revealing in spurts fleeting glimpses of the real-real Watson underneath.

"You're furry," Chuck observed.

"And you're not," Watson returned. "Everybody wonders how you manage to mate, you know."

"Actually, I don't." He observed sardonically. "There was a time when a fur coat was indeed a great mating enticement. Wouldn't matter anyway on my commissions."

"But surely we're talking on the order of millions of years since your species lost its fur in some freak aberration of evolution—"

"I was joking. So, why are three men sitting on you?"

"I haven't the faintest. I was minding my own business when they approached me uninvited."

They didn't look like thugs. In fact, they appeared quite the opposite. Hardly more than teenagers, each wore black, pressed pants, a clean, white shirt, and a thin black tie. Their hair was trimmed Donny Osmond style, and, although visibly upset, the closest they came to cursing was to cry out "Damn," as in "Damn him back to Hades!"

Chuck was beginning to get the picture. A fourth young man stood by, frantically flipping through a thick book covered in black leather.

"You seem to have riled up some missionaries."

"Missionaries . . . has Vragbushlingtit dropped me into Africa?"

"There's a sizable sub-culture that believes the rest of us right here have sunk into pagan savagery. They probably think they need to set us straight before getting back to the original business of saving the Dark Continent. What exactly did they say to you?"

"They asked whether I had taken Jesus as my savior."

"Let me guess: you didn't have time to fabricate a story."

"Frankly, I didn't see the necessity. Why on Earth would I want to hide my religious beliefs?"

"A word of advice—you might want to study humans some more before auditioning for that part. So, how did you answer?"

"I simply explained that, considering where I come from, I can't discriminate among the prophet-followers of Earth."

"That's how you said it? 'Of Earth'?"

"Correct."

"I see."

"Did I misspeak somehow?"

"You probably made their day—their year. Hell, their life. They think they hate you, but without you, they'd be out of a job. They'd have to stop bothering people and admit that they'll just have to work things out on their own like the rest of us."

"I don't understand at all. They didn't even know me until their approach."

"I don't mean you directly—what they think you are."

"What is that?"

"What else did they say?"

"After that, they sort of looked at each other, and one of them asked whether I was indeed the one fallen from heaven."

"Oh boy."

"I was, of course, surprised that they knew of me, but I assumed that Vragbushlingtit had further violated the quarantine to—"

"Note that they said, 'heaven,' not '*the* heavens'."

"Oh dear. I think I'm beginning to see."

"Maybe I should just call the police."

"Oh gracious no! There would be no end to trouble."

"The quarantine. Right."

Chuck sighed as he watched the fourth missionary shout out a passage from his Bible:

> *"Keep sober and alert, because your enemy the devil is on the prowl like a roaring lion, looking for someone to devour. Stand up to him, strong in faith."*

The companion sitting on the left looked up, puzzled, and said, "We should stand up?"

The fourth seeker-of-truth consulted his Bible again and replied, "I think it means metaphorically."

The first three then proceeded to pinch and punch through the immaterial wavering aura to the unearthly howls of their victim, then looked back up shaking their heads.

"Let me see what I can do," Chuck said. "You should probably hide this second aura. We don't need extra complications."

"Righto, old chap."

Instantly the Watson ghost was gone. Chuck noticed that, simultaneously, the Victorian figure prostrate under the missionaries' rumps solidified, as though the aura generator had an easier time of it now. This had a disconcerting effect on the religious enthusiasts.

"Corinthians!" the young man in the middle of the sitting devil retainers shouted. "Try two-eleven!"

The reader flipped pages and then intoned:

> *"Lest Satan should get an advantage of us: for we are not ignorant of his devices."*

"Hold on!" the standing young man cried. "There's another one here." He flicked forward, nearly tearing the sheets in his haste. Running his finger down a page, he stopped:

> *"Satan himself masquerades as an angel of light."*

He stared wide-eyed at his companions as they slid their hands in fearful awe through the insubstantial projection of wool coat and pants. Glancing at each other for confirmed support, they then resumed their pummeling anew.

"Yo!" Chuck shouted, skipping down the steps.

They stopped, looking up at him in surprise. One of the defenders started to stand up but the other two pulled him back.

"What's going on here?" Chuck asked as he faced the standing warrior who had positioned himself and his Bible defiantly between this interloper and the Holy Skirmish.

"It's not what it may seem," the young man warned sternly.

Chuck hadn't made up his mind whether he was going to pretend he was coming to the aid of a defenseless, if oddly dressed and partially illusory, man, or simply try to explain the truth. Facing the stony face of this young man, though, he decided to do neither, as the former would likely lead to police, while the latter would surely meet with unassailable resistance. Although the evidence implied that these young missionaries were eminently gullible, Chuck recognized that their delusions were focused sharply in one direction only.

Instead, he remembered the Judo his uncle had tried, with little success, to teach him, where the opponent's own momentum becomes the weapon that throws him.

"What it seems," he drawled, "is that you've got old Beelzebub under butt."

Watson turned his head in alarm, but Chuck ignored him. Although the mustached face lay pressed convincingly against the sidewalk, the top-hat should have been squashed, but instead seemed to merge unobstructed into the cement.

Shoulders settling with relief, the three young men eagerly demonstrated how their hands disappeared as they slid them along their captive. The Bible reader, apparently the lead thumper, watched Chuck cautiously.

"I'm surprised the old rascal allowed himself to be caught," Chuck commented casually. "And, powerful as he is, to be held down, even."

The three sitters scrunched their brows in concern, but their leader replied, "Satan is indeed powerful, but God's will prevails over even him."

Chuck nodded. Don't push back against a shove in Judo; lean with it.

"No question. No question at all . . . ultimately. We're dealing with the here and now, though, and we're stuck smack in the middle between the two. He's a wily old bastard, and his game is temptation—as you well know."

The leader watched without commenting, waiting to see where he was going.

Chuck pressed on, pointing his chin knowingly towards the prone figure. "I'd be awfully careful with any contact, even if you think you've got the upper hand."

He remembered how the aura had stabilized when Watson removed the second image. "Your temptations are his sustenance. Notice how his form has strengthened even as we talk."

The sitters peered down and around at their captive with sudden alarm, lifting their hands as though realizing that the aura might be searing hot.

"Just who are you?" the leader demanded.

"Not one of his kind," Chuck assured, gesturing at Watson, "that's for certain." This was indeed for certain. "I stand with you as your blood brother."

He didn't give the young devotee time to probe this. Mustering serious concern, he warned, "Contact is especially dangerous for those with hands dirtied by unholy acts."

Fingers gripped the Bible, shoulders squared, and eyes squinted in defiance. "We strive to live moral lives. Our goal is to serve as examples for the wayward."

"As in anybody outside your sect," Chuck muttered, but then said loudly, "Striving is commendable, but not always sufficient."

"What is and isn't sufficient is for God to decide, not you."

"Look, I'm not here to judge you. I'm just trying to help, and I'm telling you that one of your soldiers of the faith here," he gestured towards the three who still held their hands in the air as though attempting a mutual levitation, "has, in fact, summoned the Dark Deceiver. Even now, as we speak, the soul of this transgressor is teetering at the edge of the fiery precipice from which there can be no return."

Chuck wondered for a moment if he was maybe overdoing the verbal dramatics, but decided that this was exactly the kind of authoritative rhetoric these boys were used to hearing.

The eyes of all three sitters went round with fear, and they glanced nervously at each other in silent debate. The leader glared at his flock in alarmed accusation, but then turned back to Chuck. "How do you know this?"

He shrugged. "I know it."

"Why should I believe you?"

Chuck smiled. "It's not important that you believe me. It's not your soul that's on the line."

He turned to the sitting three. "Sin is Satan's handle, you know, with which he pulls you down. Every time you go against God, the despicable clutching fingers reach a little closer to grip your heart." He nodded sagely as their heads bobbed in hypnotic sync. "Think about it: you're now actually *touching* the Evil of Evils. Do you suppose you stumbled on him by accident? Oh, no. He's come to collect his side of the bargain."

Chuck glanced at the leader, now listening raptly. This was the kind of stuff the young man lived for.

"And, what a pitiful bargain it was," Chuck continued, pacing before them now. "Brief moments of sensual pleasure traded for an eternity in hell. We've all felt the temptation, and we've all had to find strength by reaching out to God for help—"

He stopped and spun on them. "All but one of you!"

He glided his eyes across them. "How could you have sunk so low?" he mourned. "You knew that this was the most shameful, the most vile desecration you could insult God with."

He held up his hands in supplication and lifted his eyes to the stars. "Why, oh why, didn't you resist the greatest of all sins?"

He lowered his accusing gaze on them and hissed, "Masturbation!"

Time froze for an eternal second, and then, with an anguished howl in three-part harmony, the sitters leapt to their feet in unison and tore away. Tortured screams echoed among the caverns of buildings.

Chuck turned to deal with the last obstacle, but the leader's face was twisted in torment. Dropping his Bible, he clasped his hands to his face and stumbled off after his flock, weeping.

Watson got to his feet and made motions of brushing off his clothes, even though it was just a projected image swiping at air.

"Bloody good show, there," he commented appreciatively. "But, how did you know they were cleaning the musket, as they say—is that what they still say?"

"Today it would more likely be spanking the monkey or maybe choking the chicken."

The screams of the damned faded into the distance as Watson's assailants tried desperately to achieve the impossible and escape from themselves.

"How did I know?" Chuck went on. "I didn't, but it was a pretty good guess. Take four young men and mandate that they remain abstinent until they get married. Human male hormones are not something that can be argued with, however. It's either break the abstinence code or dance with the one-eyed sailor—there's another one for you, by the way."

"Hmm," Watson mulled, hand on chin. "I see."

Relieved of the stress of being sat on, the aura was now remarkably effective. Watson looked exactly like a real-life . . . well, a Watson. "You might want to think about changing your metaphorical clothes."

"Jolly right," the alien false visage replied, winking.

"And that speech script thing."

"Right-o, old chap. Bloody good suggestion. Tally-ho and all that."

"Er, you might want to think about changing that part sooner rather than—"

"I was attempting a joke."

Chuck smiled. "Good one."

What now?

Be polite.

He stuck out his hand. "Well, good luck."

Watson hesitated just a moment before he reached out and shook the proffered gesture.

It was an eerie sensation grasping something much smaller than it appeared. The alien hand Chuck shook was thin, almost frail. The fingers could have been flexible straws, and the thumb seemed to wrap all the way around the top of his hand. He was sure he felt suckers at the tip.

"Good luck with that audition," Chuck bade, releasing the handshake, "and, break a leg."

"Break my . . . leg?"

"I guess they didn't use the expression back in Dickens time. Actors are superstitious—they say the opposite so they don't jinx the performance."

"Ah, right." He shook his head, perplexed. "Mercy, it seems overwhelming."

"The expression will be included in the new language script, won't it?" Chuck offered helpfully.

"I suppose so. There's just obviously so much more to a culture than the language."

"I guess there is. But, that's exactly why you're here."

"Indeed. I am now intimately familiar with the masturbation obsessions of young men."

"Uh, another joke?"

"Sarcasm."

"Same thing. But, look—isn't that the whole point? If something about our culture doesn't seem bizarre, then you probably wouldn't need to be immersed here to learn about it."

"I suppose." The alien tipped his immaterial beaver skin top-hat and said, "Quite an astute observation," as he turned to go.

"For a median cognitive position in a primitive society?"

Watson paused, turned, and winked before walking away. But, because of a little glitch in the aura generator—or perhaps on purpose—the camouflaging illusion disappeared for a brief moment and Chuck saw the creature in all its stark, alien reality. Watson was indeed furry, resembling, vaguely, a man-size spider monkey with excellent posture.

Wrapped in a tight coil above its butt, where it would stay hidden beneath the Watson exterior, was a tapering, hairless tail. Chuck's breath caught in his throat, but then he saw that the tip was just a decorative ball, not a barbed arrow at all.

Sheesh, Chuck thought, *next, I'll be believing in ghosts.*

.

Mao's Head

The President tried to focus on the summary sheet his staff had prepared for the new Sedition Act bill, one he had hoped would trump the short-lived version a century before. The bastard Democrats had wiggled in a provision providing leniency for citizens accused of denigrating the office of the President if they admitted to being insane. He had threatened to veto it if they watered it down, and now he couldn't decide what to do.

The fact that a huge alien spaceship hovered a quarter mile overhead didn't help. In fact, he admitted to himself—but not out loud—he was just keeping himself busy so he wouldn't have to think about the damn thing.

He was supposed to be the most powerful man on Earth, and he was until they showed up.

Of course, they hadn't actually proved this yet since they hadn't done anything except sit up there, but the fact that they were still sitting there after the US Airforce had thrown everything it had at them made the point rather moot.

The door suddenly burst open and Schmidt, his Chief of Staff, stood there looking flushed.

"Sorry, Sir," he said, stepping forward to hand him a sheet of paper, "but NSA has finally deciphered their message. It turns out that something got mixed up with the equipment and the text was coming in backwards. One of the NSA guys apparently carried a printout with him into the bathroom and saw it in the mirror."

"I don't care about the technicalities," the President growled, snatching the sheet from Schmidt. "They don't do my job, and I don't expect to do theirs."

He'd found early in his career that leadership was more than just knowing things.

"What does it say?" he asked, tossing the sheet forcefully onto his desk and glaring at Schmidt. He paid his Chief of Staff to tell him things, not hand him sheets of paper.

"They want the remains of their colleagues."

The President held his glare steady as he processed this information. "What the hell are you talking about?"

"From that spaceship that . . . um." Schmidt glanced around, then continued in a whisper. ". . . that crashed back in 1947 near Roswell, New Mexico. You know, it was in the transition briefing reports you read when you took office."

The President's confident glare never wavered. He remembered that part of the report, but when they wrote about aliens, he'd thought they meant Mexicans. He remembered wondering when Mexico had gotten spaceships, but he wasn't fool enough to ask. Good thing he hadn't.

"Why the hell would they come all the way to Earth for some decades-old dead bodies?"

"Well, Sir, that's sort of the problem. You see, those alien bodies we found at the crash site . . . well, apparently they weren't actually dead."

"They weren't? Did we kill them during, er, questioning?"

"No. The Army assumed that they were dead when they found the crash site. Most of them weren't even in one piece. These aliens, though, claim that they can regenerate themselves, but they need, well, all the pieces."

"Huh, no kidding."

Something about this made the President uneasy. When people died, they were supposed to stay dead. Hell, how could you run a country when people could just pop back any time? Jesus, you'd be looking over your shoulder every second, wondering who was going to rise up next to spill some more beans. What a mess the world would be—

"They're pretty upset about the dissections," Schmidt cautioned, interrupting his worry.

"Eh? Hell, they must know we have scientists. That's what scientists do."

"Yes, well, they say that if we give them all the pieces they might let it go. They'll have to think about it."

"Sounds like good news."

He was already spinning the press story in his head: *Wielding his no-nonsense approach that Americans love so much, the President convinced the aliens to spare the Earth.* That sounded too weak. . . . *the President strong-armed the aliens into accepting a truce. In exchange, America will only give up* . . . Hmm, don't want to let the cat out of the bag. *America will deliver all the stem-cell embryos.*

There, kill two pesky birds with one stone.

"Er, excuse me, Sir, but there is a small problem."

"That's why I hired you. There's always a problem. What is it this time?"

"I contacted the hidden facility at Area 51, and they say they've located all the alien pieces but one."

"Do you think these bastards hovering up there blocking the sun will notice?"

"Well, er, the missing piece is the head of what we think was the crashed ship's captain."

"Yikes!"

"Exactly, Sir. I'm afraid this may be a deal-breaker. I have an idea, though."

"Of course you do. That's why I hired you. What is it?"

"I think that President Nixon may have given it to Mao Tse-tung."

"I knew that twerp was cracked. A blemish on the ass of the Republican Party."

"Yes, Sir. I remembered from the transition briefing that Nixon had a special Air Force jet follow him on his historic visit to China. He took the moon rocks along for Mao with him on Air Force One, but apparently decided at the last minute that the rest of Mao's gifts should come separately. Haldeman's diary entry for that day read: *the Chief said he was 'creeped out' having 'that damned mummy head' around*."

"Huh. Everybody probably thought he was talking about Tip O'Neill."

"Exactly, Sir. There's one other piece of evidence I found. After Nixon's visit, Mao is quoted as saying, 'China gave the world writing, gunpowder, and toilet paper, and all the Americans bring back are some rocks and a capitalist-deformed face'."

"Let me guess: we thought all along that Mao was talking about Kissinger."

"You got it, Sir."

"You think we can get the head back?"

"The Chinese have joined the ranks of capitalist-pigs; I'm sure we can negotiate something."

ж ж ж

The President was dozing and woke with a start to find his Chief of Staff standing in the doorway. "Jesus! Don't you ever knock?"

"Er, I just did, Sir."

"Whatever. What have you got? Good news, I hope. The Second Lady is driving me nuts about that huge saucer—says it's an eyesore, and vehemently does NOT want our term to be known as the one that oversaw the end of the world. I wish to hell I could get her to stop referring to it as 'our' term in office."

"Right, Sir," Schmidt agreed. "Uh, I do indeed have some good news. Beijing claims that they have tracked down the alien head."

"Excellent! Let's heave it up there and get those ugly little bastards out of our spacious skies."

"Um, it's not quite that simple, Sir."

"Never is with the Chinese. Well, I don't pay you to handle just the simple problems."

"Er, actually, Sir, you don't pay me at all. My salary is drawn from the Federal Executive Office budget."

"Can I fire you any time I want?"

"Um, right. Good point. Anyway, it seems that Mao used the head for years as part of his sex-play with his peasant girls—thousands of them, apparently. The official position of the People's Congress is that he used it to scare them as a tease—telling them that the head represented the only possible result of Imperialist Capitalist culture. The unofficial version, though, admits that the shriveled up alien head probably made his rotting green teeth less ugly by contrast."

The President was rolling the tips of his fingers across his clean, empty desk. "Tell you what, Schmidt: add the details to Wikipedia, and maybe I'll read it someday. So, can we get the goddamn head or not?"

"Right. Sorry, Sir. Beijing wants to trade it."

"For what? Some blow-up dolls?"

"Er, actually—you're not going to like this—they want California."

The President sprang to his feet, throwing his chair back with a crash. "Is this a joke?"

He knew it wasn't. The Chinese sense of humor was about as developed as his own nurturing feminine side.

"No, Sir. Apparently they feel that they hold a very favorable bargaining position."

"All they've got is a goddamn mummy head!"

"As they put it, Sir, 'Advanced aliens are about to crap on America, and Washington is squatting right under their ass.' They made some other points as well—"

"I get the picture," he assured, waving his hand. "Hell—can't we offer them some money?"

"We already owe them over four trillion dollars. In reality, they pretty much own America; they're just asking for part of the deed."

The President of the Mortgaged-States-of-America raised himself tall and stared off presidentially for a few seconds at the wall. It wasn't often that he was called to make truly difficult decisions.

"Tell them they can have San Francisco," he said, finally turning to Schmidt. "See if they'll go for that."

His Chief of Staff looked at him a moment, and then nodded and left.

The President shrugged. Hell, he'd already lost the gay vote when he squashed the bill that would have established the gay-only Army corps.

The President paced the Oval Office. Walking back and forth across the eagle on the floor normally calmed him. He imagined that the great bird lying there with its wings outstretched was pleading for mercy. It wasn't that he enjoyed withholding mercy, he just wanted a little pleading first.

It didn't work today, though; not even when he made a point to step firmly on the olive branch. They'd given the aliens their goddamned head, but the mile-wide saucer still floated above him ready to crap on the greatest nation on Earth.

He heard footsteps, and Schmidt rushed in, looking smug.

"What the hell are you smiling about?" the President growled.

He hated it when somebody was happier than him.

His Chief of Staff jolted into his mode of serious concern. "NSA has decoded their latest communication. Turns out that the aliens started sending the messages non-reversed, and it took our guys a while to figure that out . . . sorry, Sir," Schmidt apologized when he saw his boss's glare. "The aliens haven't left because they found something of ours inside the head."

The President stared at Schmidt a moment and then slapped his hand down with a bang on his empty desk. "That head is going to be the end of me yet! By damn, it's going to be my Nixon Watergate!"

He could see that Schmidt was having an unsuccessful time hiding a smirk.

"What the *hell* is so funny!"

"Sir, it's just odd that you should bring up Nixon. You see, the thing they found inside the head is evidently one of Nixon's tape recorders. He apparently hid it in there hoping to spy on Mao. The head was sort of his own little Trojan Horse."

"Holy hell," the President muttered, taking his seat heavily. "All this time . . . I wonder if—"

"Nixon screwed up, though," Schmidt continued. "He must have accidentally turned it on too soon. According to the aliens, the whole tape is him and Kissinger talking together in China the night before they met Mao. On the snippet that the aliens sent along as proof, Nixon is asking Kissinger how he gets all the women."

The President leaned back and stared at his presidential wall. "Well, if that doesn't beat all . . ." He looked back at Schmidt.

His Chief of Staff anticipated the question. "The aliens cut it off before Kissinger answered. I think it was on purpose."

"So," he said rising slowly to face his fate. "Is this the end? Are they going to destroy the Earth?"

Schmidt looked confused a moment, then shook his head. "No. They're asking if we want the tape back. They're willing to trade for it."

The President felt a wash of relief, followed immediately by hot cheeks at his mistake. "Of course, of course. I'm sure we can come up with some appropriate offering to satisfy them, some trifle of history—the bullet that killed Lincoln, perhaps."

"Er, I'm afraid they already have something in mind, Sir."

With slow drama, the President raised one eyebrow into an imperious arch. It was the move that some say won him the Kansas City debate.

"They, uh," Schmidt began, then swallowed before continuing. "Sir, they want San Diego."

"What?"

He'd been to San Diego. It was really nice. Not many titty bars, but the people seemed real happy and friendly.

"They know that the Chinese got all of California north of Burbank," Schmidt explained, "and they see a precedence."

"I don't get it. Why San Diego?"

"Well, Sir, I don't know if you remember, but there was this whacko cult that committed mass suicide, thinking they were hitching a ride on a comet."

"They bit the collective dust in a place called Rancho Santa Fe. I remember because it sounded like a Mexican Restaurant."

"It's a suburb. Well, it turns out that they weren't whackos at all. The aliens feel bad about it. They were supposed to pick them up, but got the dates mixed up. Apparently they were having problems with backwards transmissions even then. It's not clear if they want to make it up to the victims' families, or wipe the whole city off the map to get rid of the evidence."

"Shit!" The President exclaimed, unconsciously letting his famous arch relax back to a natural grouchy scowl. "If we don't nip this in the bud, the country will be whittled down to just Washington and the Jersey Turnpike! I'll have to trade Airforce One in for a hybrid with the Presidential Seal on the side!"

"I agree, Sir. It's just an old tape—probably smells bad too."

"Right. Just an old tape."

Ah, but not just any old tape, The President thought as his eyebrow inched back up of its own accord. He made fun of the old rascal like everybody else, but secretly he admired the doughty Vietnam warlord. MacArthur, Patton, Nixon—these were the pillars of the last century. And here, practically falling headlong into his lap was the old dog himself conversing casually with Kissinger, no less. Why, he could lock the door, play the tape, and pretend it was three great leaders just having a good old chat.

"Did San Diego vote for me?" he asked.

"It was a red city," Schmidt replied.

"Bright red, or just pink?"

"I don't know, Sir."

The difference between great leaders and Democrats was character fiber. And the measure of that fiber was the willingness to make difficult decisions and not pussy-foot around about it.

The President slapped his hand down on his desk, and the impact shot away across the empty, polished surface to fill the room with the resonating call of a historical turning point.

"By damn, tell the little bastards they have a deal."

The Iceman Goeth

Dr. Bradoski was temporarily dead. Unfortunately, since it had been well over two centuries since he'd stopped breathing, even he, who had stilled his own heart, would probably have admitted that, as a descriptive term, temporary was becoming somewhat untenable.

Twenty-three decades before, the esteemed climatologist had stood on top of a half mile of millennia-old ice and reviewed his options. This close to the South Pole, the sun in April hovered barely above the horizon both day and night. His American team arbitrarily defined "day" as when the sullen orb rode the horizon a thousand miles away over the Billinghausen Sea, in the direction of America. "Night" was when it circled around towards Australia. Ninety-three miles to the south was the axis of the Earth's rotation. North was life.

Every way he looked at it he was going to die within the next six hours, but there were still options. There were always options; it came down to probability. Engineers typically design systems to be tolerant of single-point failures, since enhanced tolerance was often prohibitively expensive. Also, the chance that two fatal failures would occur simultaneously was usually small enough to ignore. As though to demonstrate the truth of this, three serious mistakes were required for Dr. Bradoski to finally spell his own doom.

His first mistake had been to allow his subordinate to return alone to Home Base, this against International Arctic Exploration Association rules. If either left, they were both supposed to leave. He had never really cared for the subordinate, and had grown to actually despise the troublesome young man who questioned every decision. At the conclusion of their final argument, he'd been glad to watch the backup snow rover fishtail away on its sixty-mile journey north.

Left on his own at the observation outpost, the doctor should have been more vigilant than ever about maintenance. This was his second mistake. He knew how to fix the brake failsafe on the primary rover; in fact, he'd already done it once back at Home Base. It was just so damn cold out there. He was confident that a warming trend would arrive in a day or two, and he'd told himself that he'd get to it then, when the temperature might climb above sixty below.

The third mistake was the dramatic one, the kind with enough action and noise to rivet your attention in rapt awe at the obvious consequences. He'd just returned from morning readings and had left the snow rover, nothing much more than a snow-mobile modified to operate in sub-zero temperatures, running outside the hut. This was routine, since he would be leaving in another hour for the rest of the collections, and if he shut it down, he'd just have to connect the umbilical power, which kept the machine's engine from completely freezing up.

Leaving the rover in gear was not routine, however, and he didn't mean to. It was just so damn cold that he sometimes wasn't careful. From inside the hut, where he was removing his frost-encased gloves, he watched in alarm through the double-paned Plexiglas window as the machine lurched when the parking brake gave way under the strain. That would have been the end of it had the failsafe brake been working, but instead, his only means of transport surged away out of view. Five seconds later, a metal-tearing crash pierced the Antarctic silence. The hut went dark, and the hum of the circulation fans slumped to a whisper and then died altogether, leaving just the whistle of Antarctic wind inexorably drawing away the heat from the slight structure.

Outside, he found disaster. The rover had leapt forward directly into the utility shed. A flimsy construction, the shed had torn like paper, and the rover had crashed through, cutting the methane tank line and disabling the fuel cell assembly before breaking one of its tread links, disabling itself. In five heartbeats, his third and last mistake had left him with no heat, no power for his radio, and no means to escape.

He tried contacting Home Base with the rover, but the small radio was short-range and only returned static to his panicked shouts. He then attempted to use the rover's lithium battery in place of the fuel-cell, but the main system was 24-Volts, and the rover's 12-Volts didn't even light up the radio display in the hut. To top off the bad day turning lethal, he somehow managed to short the lithium batteries' leads, yanking his hands back from the red-hot wire before the plastic battery cube burst open with a defeated pop.

It was then that Dr. Bradoski accepted that he was dead. The pop of the lithium battery self-destructing was the herald of his countdown. Heat, from the hut and from his body, was leaking into the Antarctic eternal dusk, and in a matter of hours his metabolic processes would loose the battle. Ruining the rover's lithium battery would have counted as a fourth mortal mistake, except that he was doomed anyway.

The hut was already getting noticeably colder. Had he not ruined the rover's battery, he could have started the motor and connected his weather suit, which drew heat from the engine when riding. As it was, the best he could do was pull on his two sweaters and a dirty sweatshirt that his subordinate had left behind, and climb back into his weather suit. He'd bought himself maybe another hour, and he was out of options.

At least, he was out of options that included living.

Dr. Bradoski knew that his fellow scientists would eventually investigate when he failed to report in, but he would be dead long before that. Well, then, he decided, so be it. He shuddered at the very thought, though. It was a long-shot ticket, but the only game in town.

He dove headlong into his task with fierce determination, fearing that he might have a change of heart. First, from the crumpled utility shed he dragged a plastic shipping container that had been used for transporting various observation instruments. Three feet on each edge, it was just large enough for his purpose. It wasn't water-tight, but he decided that this didn't matter, at Antarctic temperatures, containers tended to be self-sealing. Warming himself as best he could in the inexorably cooling hut, he then headed off directly south, towards the pole, dragging the large plastic box behind him. Topping a small ridge only a few hundred feet from the station, he managed to proceed another hundred yards. He decided not to go any farther, since his next load would be significantly more difficult to manhandle.

He made it back to the hut and slapped feeling back into his hands and feet while contemplating his next move. He needed something with a lot of metal, but not so heavy that he couldn't move it. He settled on the fuel cell assembly. Although fairly large, it was mostly a honeycomb of fuel chambers. It took him three returns to the hut for warm-ups before he had the assembly disconnected and emptied. He then began the long, difficult job of dragging it over the ridge to join the waiting box. The first attempt, before he was forced back to the hut with numb hands, saw it proceed all of four feet from the shed. At this rate he would obviously never get the assembly to the box before the hut lost all heat.

He needed help. The problem was that the corners kept digging into the snow. As kids in Philadelphia, they would use garbage can lids as saucer sleds. He rummaged around inside the station and found the shipping box's plastic top. With generous amounts of grunting and prodigious amounts of swearing, he maneuvered the fuel cell assembly up and onto it. Warming up in the ever-colder hut took disturbingly longer, but he was then able to drag the makeshift sled nearly to the top of the ridge before staggering back numb and feeling dumb with fatigue.

Yard by yard, he pushed and pulled and shoved and cursed the metal monster farther from the remote station. Each trip back to the hut was less rewarding, and it seemed now to provide no heat whatsoever, just a way to get out of the knife-cold wind. Finally, his fingers remained numb no matter how much he slapped and rubbed them, and he knew that he had moved the fuel-cell assembly as far as it was going to go. It was still fifty feet from where he had left the packing box, and it was a testament to the power of hypothermia that it took him a minute to realize that he could simply move the box back this small remaining distance.

He needed to make one last trip to the hut. Inside, his breath flowed from his mouth in billowing clouds that disappeared instantly in the bone-dry air. With fingers that felt like hot-dogs attached to stumps of long-forgotten fingers he scrawled out the note he'd been composing in his mind the last hour, and placed it prominently on the folding table they had used as a desk. Then for the last time, he left the cozy little outpost that had been his home these last few months, closing the door carefully behind him. The wind felt like a hand slapping his face, and what he had thought was cold air inside the hut now seemed balmy as the inside of his nose seemed to tinkle with stinging shards of ice.

Rummaging through the twisted confusion of the shed, he found the propane torch and extra canisters and headed off to his new, simpler home. As he climbed the ridge, he looked back at the trail he'd made in the snow on his trips back and forth. The same warming system would bring new snow the next day—plenty to cover his tracks.

He had to move fast now. It would be bad luck indeed if he succumbed to the pole's frozen grip before his final preparation. He threw armloads of hard-packed snow into the plastic box and melted them with the jumbo-flame torch. He'd worried that it wouldn't have the BTUs to best the intense freeze of the Antarctic's core, and he was relieved to see the snow melt and the water level rise in the box. The first canister yielded six inches of water. With just two canisters left, panic swelled a moment when he realized he could fill only half the box. His brain seemed to be infused with thick molasses that addled and muffled each thought. He forced himself to concentrate, however, and, as though slowly recognizing the form of a friend emerging from fog, understood that a half-full container was more than enough. The water would be sharing the volume of the box.

He almost made a last mistake, but his slow-motion mind remembered to shut off the torch before that last of the propane was gone. He could see the heat still radiating from the nozzle. As though no longer at home in his own body, he watched with mild wonderment as his hand grasped the metal tube. He felt nothing. No, somewhere off in the distance, somewhere where he used to live, he felt vague pain, and then he smelled the acrid stench of burning flesh.

He let go. That was stupid. But the heat was so seductive.

Heat. He had to let go of the whole concept. Heat was something from a long-ago past.

He saw that a skim of ice was forming on the water. He stirred the box with the torch so that all the water would be the same freezing temperature. This was important. He had decided this long ago—when he was still part of the living world. Why? Did he still know? Yes—speed in reaching an overall reduced body temperature was critical. The doctor he used to be had known this, and he trusted that man.

What next? He didn't know. What did that doctor want him to do? He should have written it down for him. No, he remembered, but it seemed crazy. He had to trust the doctor. He stepped into the box and was mildly surprised that he didn't even feel the cold water. There was just enough room to crouch and lay down in a fetal position.

He still had the torch in his hand. He was supposed to do something with that. He remembered that much. He had an image of him sucking on it. It came to him what the doctor wanted him to do. He turned the wheel and heard the hiss of propane. He was going scuba diving, and this was his air tank. Part of him was surprised that people could breathe propane instead of oxygen, but the doctor, impatient, just as he'd always been impatient with his subordinate, explained that it was necessary to keep his lungs from filling with water. That wouldn't do. It would cause structural damage to the delicate tissue as the water froze that even an advanced far-future medicine might not be able to repair.

He put the nozzle, already bitterly cold, into his mouth. The propane was not unpleasant. He breathed deeply, and felt a warm blanket flutter down around him.

One more thing! For God's sake, don't forget the last thing! He squatted down and curled into a ball, barely feeling the icy water envelop him, filling the box and sloshing over.

He was ready to leave. But just as the veil of sleep settled peacefully over him, one final worry flitted across his conscience like the shadow of a leaf blowing in the wind. For the barest moment he feared that he'd forgotten the note. But no, he remembered placing it next to the radio, misleading his companions that he'd headed north on foot, that he was going to try to walk to Home Base. At all costs he had to prevent them from searching the area and finding him here, frozen in his cube of ice. Even if he had explained what he was attempting with this one-in-ten-thousand long shot, they could never willingly leave him behind. Laws of man would surely demand a proper autopsy, and then he would be good and dead. His world did not yet have the technology to thaw a man and restore him to life. But perhaps, just maybe, a future world would. Maybe, just maybe, some advanced future civilization, drawn by the odd concentration of metal of the fuel cell assembly, would come to investigate.

Maybe, just maybe.

ж ж ж

Braden and Paully skimmed low across the snow ridges of the Antarctic. They traveled along at near Mach one, but the only indication of their passing was a mighty swoosh of air and dust devils of blown snow in their wake. They were taking a break from their construction jobs at the Amundsen Estates condo site just a few klicks from the busy complex that crowded the geographic South Pole. The car belonged to the developer, and they weren't supposed to be out for a joy ride.

One of the sensors beeped.

"What?" Braden barked.

"*I've detected metal,*" a pleasant voice informed.

Braden looked at Paully. "Details," Paully ordered.

"*A small structure constructed from formed and bent metal. From design and accumulated ice layers, I estimate that it is between two-hundred-fifty to three hundred years old.*"

Braden whistled. "That's twenty-first century. Probably left by early explorers—maybe even Byrd himself!"

Paully snorted. "Byrd came around 1900, you idiot. Three hundred years ago there were only science expeditions here. This is probably a piece of their equipment."

Braden gave Paully a knowing look. They both understood that this was a prime find. An early twenty-first scientific artifact could make them rich. It would have been perfectly preserved here in the eternal freeze, beyond the reach of the metal-eating bacteria that had forced the world to give up iron and aluminum for synthetic building materials. Whatever it was, it might even still work! They could sell it to the Smithsonian!

"Investigate," Paully told the car.

They made a wide turn and within a few minutes were hovering over a nondescript expanse of snow. "Report," Paully said.

"*The metal artifact is most likely an early period fuel cell powering system—*"

"Fuel cell?" Braden cut in.

"*This was a relatively efficient system used for converting hydro-fuel into electrical energy. It was popular for a short period as an alternative to chemical batteries. It was quickly abandoned when vacuum energy was harnessed.*"

"No moving parts, then."

"*Correct.*"

Braden sighed. "I was hoping for an operating piston engine."

Paully was peering at the 3-D image the car had displayed on the window screen. "It could still be worth a lot—it sounds like rare technology."

"*I can now see another object close by.*"

Braden looked hopeful again. "What does this look like?"

"*A frozen man.*"

"What!"

"*It appears to be a man curled into a plastic box. The box contains ice. It seems that the box was filled with water which later froze.*"

Braden and Paully exchanged surprised looks. "A bizarre burial ritual?" Braden offered.

"I don't think so," Paully said. "They started cremating their dead by then. Maybe a murder victim?"

"I don't think so," the car countered. *"I believe that this man was alive when submerged in the water. I perceive a metal canister inserted in the man's mouth—what I presume was a breathing apparatus."*

Paully shook his head in confusion. "This is bizarre. What's going on?"

"I have a hypothesis," the car offered. *"This man may have been attempting to preserve his body."*

Paully nodded. "That's right, they used to freeze people to preserve them ... so, maybe he was stranded here, and this was his only option? He knew that he wouldn't thaw this close to the pole until someone found him."

The car didn't reply, apparently assuming that this was a rhetorical question. The two men sat pondering this while the car waited patiently for further directions.

"Let's take the fuel cell and go," Braden finally said.

"Leave the man?"

"They'll thaw him—they thawed all those people who froze themselves in the twentieth century. Remember the problems?"

Paully nodded. "Legal battles over property ownership."

"That's right. The courts finally decided in favor of the corpse-sicles. They took over property they'd owned over a century before. People lost their homes. This man will claim that the fuel cell belongs to him."

Paully sat chewing his lip. "It's not like we would be killing him. He's already dead."

Braden waited for his friend to decide.

ж ж ж

Fifteen minutes later the car sped off towards Amundsen Estates. In the luggage compartment, hot air whistled across the precious cargo, drying it before it began to corrode. They'd catch hell for taking the car, but it was worth it. If the foreman gave them trouble, they could afford to quit now.

The two friends had known each other a long time. They trusted each other. Each could count on the other to never again mention the Iceman.

God Takes Another Swing

ARC-1 was invisible to David, even as the shuttle pilot console insisted that it was closing no more than two klicks ahead. This was mostly an electronic supposition, since the reflective sphere was equally adept at deflecting 99 percent of the docking radar. The satellite station's synchronous orbit was now passing through the Earth's shadow so that the uncountable stars surrounding it blazed with almost painful brilliance. Dead ahead he finally discerned a gathering of star pinpoints where the sphere concentrated the reflections at its center. A grand-daddy mirror-ball.

Had he thought about it, he would have anticipated the visual novelty, but for the last eighteen months he'd been engrossed with the orbital stability subsystem, and the mirrored outer shell had always been just one of a thousand other abstract line details in the 3D model. Besides, the sophisticated surface—reflective to so much of the electromagnetic spectrum—wasn't intended for stealth, but simply refrigeration.

He'd never expected to see his handiwork in operation, and was pleasantly surprised when McGathers had told him to come up, promising to reimburse him for the astounding cost of the shuttle rental. He couldn't imagine why the irascible old man would want him on site, but then again, it was impossible to predict the motives of a man who had essentially blown his entire famously substantial fortune on a—let's face it, pretty quirky—abstract benefit for humankind.

And, McGathers was not a man who David envisioned as caring two hoots about humankind.

The "1" in the station's title presumed that it was just the first Archival Repository of Chromosomal samples. David wasn't sure, though, what number two would contain, since this one already included genetic sample of two hundred thousand species of plants and nearly a million species of animals, from eight hundred individual species of coral to over five thousand mammals. Hell, the three hundred-meter sphere contained replicable seeds of over eighty percent of all life on Earth.

Maybe number two was going to be a backup. If so, he wasn't sure how the eccentric ex-billionaire intended to pay for it. Also, if there was going to be backup redundancy, why had he been told to spare no expense to design an orbital control system that was both autonomous and fail-proof at 99.99 percent confidence for an operating period of no less than a hundred years?

David, along with the rest of the world, suspected that the old curmudgeon knew something they didn't, but if so, he wasn't talking.

Ten minutes later, David pulled himself through the inner portal door and bumped head-first into McGather's stomach.

"Watch it!" the grizzled old man grouched, shoving David aside and pulling himself through the hatch.

"Where are you going?" David squeaked.

"I have to make a run to New York," McGather explained, making a deft one-eighty turn inside the small lock chamber. "In the meantime, He wants to talk to the two of you," he added, reaching out to close the hatch door.

"What 'He?' What two of us?" David bleated, grabbing the hatch door.

"The 'He' he. Who else? Tony's in the lounge waiting for you."

He'd seen a Tony on the project rosters.

"Tony the biologist?"

"No. Tony the Medieval nudist alchemist. Now let go of the door before I sock you one," the wiry septuagenarian ordered, slamming it shut with a thud.

"But . . ."

There had been no other shuttles parked at the giant sphere when he'd arrived.

He found his way to the tiny galley and on through to the small common lounge, working from his mental map of the 3D model. He was surprised to find a woman floating cross-legged staring out the only port window of the facility, positioned to face the fixed disc of Earth, now dark except for a knife-sharp crescent of sunlight refracting through the sliver shell of atmosphere.

"I, uh . . ." he started.

The woman deftly spun herself around using her forefinger against the edge of the port. She had short, dark hair, dark eyes, almond skin, and a lightness of spirit, at least so it seemed to David as she cocked her left eyebrow curiously at seeing him. At the same time, she seemed distracted, as though listening to a Bach concerto that he couldn't hear.

"I, was, um . . ." He tried again, "I was expecting Tony."

The corner of her mouth lifted into a grin worn down with repetition to a stub. "You've found her," she confirmed, straightening her back and extending her arms in a wake-up stretch.

"Tony's a . . ."

"She."

"Why don't you spell it with an 'i'?"

"Why don't you wear a tag on your shirt that says 'man'?"

"Er, fair enough. So, I assume McGather summoned you up as well. Before rushing off and leaving us stranded here, he mumbled that somebody wanted to talk to us. Who else is here?"

Tony's stubby grin widened into a radiant smile. "You don't know?"

"Know what?"

Into the recycled air of the lounge she called, "Do you want to tell him?" She waited a few seconds, staring blankly at the wall, then shrugged. "He must be out at the moment."

"Who? How do you step out for a moment from an orbital station?"

She looked him straight in the eye and he almost forgot his consternation under her soulful gaze.

"Do you believe in God?" she asked.

"Well, sure. I mean, not the kind of God with a long beard who appears above the clouds and booms out commands. More like a deist God who permeates the whole universe, in a way who IS the whole universe—"

"You were right the first time."

"What are you talking about?"

"He hasn't appeared above the clouds for centuries, but that was him."

David just stared at her as she watched him confidently. Was she joking, or had an undetected solar flare scrambled her brains? He felt the skin along his spine tingle as he had the sudden thought that maybe the old man had been escaping her delusions, leaving him as a decoy.

"It was He who told McGrath to build this station," she explained.

"God told him to blow his whole fortune to build this. You're serious."

"Totally. After He destroys all the life on Earth, this station will be used to re-populate the planet."

David blinked. "This is, like, some modern Noah's Ark?"

"What's the name of the station?"

He squinted at her cautiously. He probably shouldn't be encouraging her. "The Archival Repository—"

"No, the acronym."

"You mean . . . no, no—wait a second. The Noah's version had a 'k,' not a 'c.' The similarity must be a coincidence."

"He says that coincidences are what happens when He's not watching."

"Sometimes he's watching, and sometimes he's not?"

"He can't be everywhere at once."

"I thought that's what being God is all about."

"People like to believe that sort of thing."

"Look . . . Tony"—he wasn't sure he'd ever get used to the name not belonging to a man—"if this is a joke, I think it's gone far enough."

"It's not a joke. Well, okay, in a macabre universe-perspective sort of way I guess it is. Particularly considering the irony that just three years ago the Western Alliance nixed the funding for the Asteroid Patrol. Otherwise, Man might have actually trumped God's hand. How embarrassing would that have been?"

"What the hell are you talking about?"

"There is no such thing as hell. That was an idea that we made up. He thought it was pretty inventive, though, and decided it could be a useful stick, so he let it ride. On the other hand, there were apparently times when He thought he *had* created hell. Armenia, the Holocaust, and disco come to mind—"

"*Asteroids*—what about the *asteroids!*"

"Oh, there's one heading for the Earth. That's why we need ARC-1. I told you that."

He stared at her. She gazed back serenely. She didn't look insane. That might not mean much, though.

He shook his head, trying to clear the spell her charm and beauty were casting. "Look, you stay right here. I'm going to the com station and give McGathers a call—"

He was interrupted by a whooshing sound and he gasped. There, floating in the air like a cheesy special-effect alien in the original Star Trek series, was God's grandfatherly head, white flowing beard and all. "Sorry," the head said. "I had to make sure McGathers nav computer wouldn't let him come back."

"What the hell . . . !" David cried, paddling backwards ineffectually in the air.

"Calm down," Tony soothed. "I had the same reaction."

God's head couldn't be his imagination. Even though it was semi-transparent, the details—minute, precise wrinkles and eyebrow hairs that bristled in sea-urchin sweeps—were far beyond his mind's own ability to fabricate. He clasped his hands over his face and whimpered.

"Hey!" God's basso profundo voice admonished, "don't make me sorry I chose you!"

He peeked through his fingers. The voice, even though heavy with authority and admonition, also conveyed a trustworthy evenness—a consistency and stability you could count on. A guy who knew what he was doing. This was exactly what you'd expect God's voice to be like. At least, when you were seven years old sitting in church under the stained glass windows.

"Chose me for what?" David asked, slowly lowering his hands.

The head remained in place, but the eyes scanned sideways towards Tony. "You haven't filled him in?"

"He knows the basics," she replied.

The eyes slid back towards him. "So, what part of re-populating the Earth don't you understand?"

"That's, er, a pretty old joke—hey, did you make up the original?"

"I don't joke."

"Right." The image of an asteroid hurtling towards the planet caused his heart to flutter. He shook his head. "Why?"

"Joking is a sophomoric form of humor. Just because humans—"

"No. I mean, why are you going to destroy the Earth?"

It occurred to him that God was indeed not omniscient, otherwise he would have read his mind.

"I'm not destroying the Earth; just all life."

"Whew. I feel so much better."

"Do you really want to joke around with God?"

"So, why? Why destroy all life?"

"That's not actually the goal, just an unfortunate side-effect. It's the only way to get rid of all the people."

"You—God—want to get rid of *all* the people?"

"We don't really need this visual," God said in answer, and the floating head disappeared.

"Visual manifestations are tiring for him," Tony whispered.

"But he's God! He can destroy all life, yet he gets tired being a ghost-head?"

Tony shrugged.

"I'm still here, you know," God's voice said, seeming to come from everywhere at once.

"So, why? Why destroy everybody?"

"It's a long story."

"I should hope so! I'd hate to think you do that sort of thing without taking time to consider all the angles."

"Are you questioning God's methods?"

David started to apologize, but caught himself. Either this whole thing was some kind of elaborate hoax, or God really was going to destroy all life on Earth. Either way, he had little to lose. "Yeah! I am questioning your methods. What the hell!"

"You're not going to like the explanation."

"How can it be worse than the consequence?"

"Good point. Okay, the problem started a couple of hundred thousand years ago when H-sapiens got ahead of the hominid part of the program—"

"What program?"

"Why, everything."

"Everything, as in the entire universe?"

"Of course not. Everything as in the whole Earth. That's my domain. I've got the rest of the Solar System as well, but that's pretty much just a big, barren backyard."

"Huh. I sort of figured that God would be . . . well, God—Lord of everything—the whole shebang."

"That's ridiculous when you take the barest moment to think about it. How could one intelligent entity keep tabs on the entire universe? Do you have any idea how big that is?"

"So, you're telling me that the Earth is essentially all there is—the only important part of the whole universe. We were the center of it all along, at least in a metaphorical sense."

"Now you're embarrassing me."

"I'm embarrassing *you*?"

"You're my creation—accidental or otherwise—and when you say dumb things like that, it reflects on me."

"How is it dumb? If we're the only planet in the universe that warrants God's attention—"

"There's your problem. What makes you think I'm the only God? Sheesh! That would make for an awfully lonely place. No, there's a bountiful gaggle of us, each with their own show planet."

"Show planets? That sounds like a dog show."

God gave no response.

"Are you saying—oh, no!" David groaned, glancing at Tony, who was listening curiously, as though hearing this part for the first time. "Don't tell me the whole Earth has been just some kind of competition entry."

"A dud one at that," God finally resumed.

"That's why the asteroid?"

"Humans have metastasized. I need a systemic sweep. Leave just a few, and before you know it, the buggers will re-populate the whole planet. Before you can blink, they'll be re-building vacation condos on Tahiti. It's a long shot, but I still have a dozen million years before the competition deadline."

"And you need ARC-1 for a head start."

"Oh, goodness, it would be stunningly impossible otherwise. After all, it took over a billion years just to progress from prokaryotes to eukaryotes."

"Pardon?"

"Eukaryotic cells have nuclei," Tony explained. "Bacteria are prokaryotes."

David's head felt like the time he overloaded on hash and amphetamines together on a dare. "But . . . I mean, we can't be all *that* bad! You could still show us!"

"I'd be laughed off the cosmic stage. I'd get you all primped up, and as soon as my back was turned, you'd be throwing nuclear bombs at each other."

"We could learn! We're great learners!"

"I've tried that already. It only got me in deeper. A few thousand years ago, when I finally accepted that I had a real doozy of a problem developing, I decided to play my trump card. I had been suspicious about the Sapiens from the very beginnings in Africa, and so I had added a collar."

David involuntarily reached up to feel his neck for some subtle imprint.

"I mean figuratively," God barked impatiently. "You call it religious yearning."

"You *made* us worship you?"

"I made you *listen* to me. *You* decided to warp it into some kind of prostrate-and-beg-for-easy-riches thing. The ambitious among you even figured out how to work it—all those shamans and priests and patriotic flag-wavers down through history. I tell you, it's downright infuriating."

"Why'd you wait this long? Why didn't you just knock them off as they sprang up? You could have eliminated a bully gene or two in the process."

"There's the rub. I couldn't. For the last couple of thousand years I've been operating under self-imposed constraint. Heck, I can hardly maintain a visual manifestation for more than a few minutes now. As I was saying, a few thousand years ago it was quite different. That's when I started seriously trying to train you Sapiens—the Old Man above the clouds bit. You're so wild-spirited, though, it just got out of hand. Before I knew it, I was parting seas and bringing plagues of locusts down on Pharaoh's heads."

"Not to mention killing all the first-born."

"Ouch. That was a misunderstanding. You've been throwing that back in my face ever since. Anyway, I knew I was stepping way outside the rules of engagement, but I was just so desperate."

"There's rules?"

"Of course. Otherwise there's no sport."

"That's why the self-imposed constraints? To make up for heavy handed miracles?"

"If I can pull this off with such a tiny smidgen of control, I might have a ghost of a chance of winning. Subtly is now the keyword. The delicate touch."

"Wiping out all life with a monster asteroid—how is that subtle or delicate?"

"We're not talking about lifting a mighty God-hand to grab a passing space-mountain like some enormous cosmic ball-game. We're looking at a total effort barely topping a few Newtons of force. Re-distribute some black carbon and white frozen ammonia judiciously around an asteroid so that the solar light pressure nudges it the tiniest little bit one way. Two thousand years later it finds itself twelve-thousand miles sideways from its original path when it passes the Earth in a near-collision encounter—except now the 'near' has been removed from the encounter."

"Two thousand years ago."

"A bit less."

"After Christ was crucified on the cross."

"What a nice boy. He was my last hope." God sighed. "Let me tell you: if Sapiens aren't bludgeoning each other over earnest call-to-arms for God and Country, you're throwing yourselves exuberantly under the wagon wheels to make a God-knows-what point, and I'm God, and I don't even know the point. Sometimes I think it's just for spite."

"So, you didn't ask him to martyr himself on the cross?"

"Now, why would I do that? Gracious, look what that led to. I have to say, though, the Catholic Church has done me one huge favor: I've never had to regret the asteroid."

"Speaking of which," David said, looking skeptically at Tony, "how do we know you're not bluffing? What if you're just trying to manipulate us somehow?"

"Well, for one thing, I never bluff. Old Lot found that one out when I exchanged his wife for a lifetime supply of salt. For another thing, it's a moot point now anyway."

The tingling along David's spine returned. "You mean, you couldn't change it even if you wanted to? But you said that your powers are self-imposed. If you really wanted to, couldn't you—"

"Close your eyes."

"Huh?"

"Close your eyes, or you'll be blinded."

"What the heck are you—"

"CLOSE THEM NOW!"

Tony was already squeezing hers shut, and she covered them with her hands for added measure. He was lucky he was looking at her at that moment, for a blast of white-hot light suddenly burst through the port window behind him, filling the lounge with an illumination that seemed to have actual substance in its hellish intensity. This was a blast that was a million times more powerful than all Earth's nuclear bombs exploding at the same instant, hotter than the surface of the sun. This was a blast from a planetoid-sized asteroid punching through the Earth's atmosphere faster than he could draw a gasp and shout, "*Shit!*" This was a blast that would have damaged his retina, yet one that was twenty-four thousand miles away.

David tried to close his eyes, but the horror and raw curiosity were overwhelming, and he turned to see. Fortunately for him the incomprehensible quantity of kinetic energy was spreading from the impact point at the speed of sound and the core temperature was dropping quickly. A slowly expanding ring of angry red fire hundreds of miles across rushed away from a white-hot center that was already fading to yellow, a mini sun kissing the planet in a death embrace. Unbelievably, he could discern geysers of molten lava streaming up and arcing over, the Earth's very blood leaking into space.

"You've punctured the very crust!" David breathed, struggling to comprehend the magnitude of the cataclysm.

"Barely," God replied calmly. "Most of what you see are crustal layers melted by the impact."

"The greater part of the damage hasn't even begun," Tony added evenly. "A natural monster form of nuclear winter will set in and last for years. The continents will freeze, but more importantly, the ocean plankton will die off, and with it, the rest of the food chain all the way up to and including humans."

David spun on her. Although she had sounded as calm as God, her face was sad. "How can you be so blase, so . . . clinical!" he shouted at her. "Don't you realize what just *happened?*"

She shrugged. "I guess I just had more time to get ready. There's nothing anybody could have done about it. We have to just swallow our grief and carry on."

"Carry *on?* Carry ON! With *what*, for God's sake?"

"Exactly," God said.

David glanced around involuntarily. He wasn't even used to a disembodied voice; how could he get used to the sudden, irreversible squashing of all known life? "What . . ."

"He means, you were right when you said for God's sake," Tony explained.

David threw out his arms dramatically, which rotated him sideways so that he had to pull himself back to face Tony. "What! Re-populate the Earth for him after he's murdered billions and billions of people—*all* of them!"

"Not quite all," God corrected.

"*Right!*" David shouted into the air. "You still have Tony and me. We're, like some modern Noah couple, or Adam and Eve."

He glanced at the only woman left in the universe, and she gazed soulfully back at him. He felt his cheeks grow warm. She was a fine specimen of womanhood—beautiful, in fact—but broaching the subject of mating and turning out human spuds together for the rest of their lives seemed way over the line. He didn't even know where she stood on gun control.

"You understand, David," God said, "that we're talking about the human embryos archived aboard ARC-1."

David's cheeks seemed to catch fire. "Of course. What the hell did you think I meant?"

Tony was grinning.

"The Earth can't even *support* life!" he shouted, glad to change the subject. "You've handily taken care of that." To Tony, he asked. "How long did you say the nuclear winter would last?"

She scrunched her brow in thought. "A year or two at the very least. Most probably the climate won't settle down for upwards of a decade."

He had the impression that she hadn't considered this until now. Her serene countenance had turned worried.

"You won't need the Earth for now," God assured. "You have an incubator. Biosphere will arrive within a month."

David had forgotten about that. It had been all over the news. Biosphere was the brainchild of Bill Gates' grandson. Like McGathers, the software magnate's descendant had a grand idea. Unlike David's boss, though, young Gates had only squandered a portion of his inherited fortune, roping in the UN Exploration Foundation to fund the majority of the cost of what had become every environmentalist's wet dream. The self-contained little world was meant to demonstrate that a properly balanced biological system, from simple oxygen-generating algae to small mammals, could be self-sustaining—anywhere. Biosphere was essentially a cruise ship-sized terrarium roaming the back alleys of the Solar System. Tooling between the lifeless wastes of the other inner planets, strutting its lifesome vigor in stark contrast to the hellish heat of Venus and the dried-up cusp of Mars, it was essentially a publicity stunt, a nose-thumbing to all the conservative Earth-hugging isolationists.

Who, David reminded himself, were now all dead.

"Biosphere is big," Tony observed, "but not nearly big enough to host all the life forms represented in ARC-1—not by a long shot."

"It won't need to," God countered, "at least, not all at one time. You'll start with the largest animals. They grow slowly. The gestation period for an elephant is nearly two years. By the time Biosphere starts getting crowded, Earth's climate will have settled enough to bring the whole circus down. Borneo is right on the equator. In a few years, it will approximate a northern tundra environment—a bit chilly, but warm enough to get the new ball rolling. Year-by-year, things will warm up, and the living tide flowing from the Biosphere nexus will spread outward in a wave of spirited rebirth."

"Very poetic," David remarked

"I've had a lot of time to think about it."

"One little problem, and it doesn't seem very God-like to have overlooked this: Biosphere was designed to float around in space, it has no means to land on a planet."

"It is God-like, though, to bring it down using methods beyond current human comprehension."

"What happened to the self-imposed 'delicate touch'?"

"You're going to bring it down for me according to my step-by-step instructions."

"Sort of like trained monkeys doing your bidding."

God didn't answer.

"Any other insightful observations?" Tony quipped.

David just snorted and shook his head. There was something about the whole thing that bothered him. Besides that fact that God had just wiped out all multi-cellular life.

"I guess the human embryos will be part of the first batch," David offered, trying to convey a casual nonchalance. "Maybe wait a year to start thawing them so that the toddlers can play horsy with the baby elephants and tigers."

He held his breath. He had the notion that the answer was possibly the most important ever to be considered in all human history.

"Actually," God replied in his usual steady voice, "humans will be introduced last. It's more orderly that way."

David nodded agreeably and glanced quickly at Tony. She was watching him closely, seeming to know something important was transpiring. "I imagine you'll do a bit of subtle genetic engineering, though, to improve the stock—repair some of the rambunctious exuberance that caused so much trouble the first time around."

"Perhaps. Look, I'm getting really tired. I think I overdid the self-imposed restraints. I'll be back in a bit. Take the time to look over the living quarters. It's your home until Biosphere arrives."

David counted slowly to twenty, staring blankly at the wall. Glancing knowingly at Tony, he called into the air, "Hey God! One more thing!"

Silence.

He hoped God really couldn't read his mind. "Listen! It's all starting to sink in, and I don't think I can take it! It's just not worth living anymore!"

He peeled away the mini tool-set he always kept strapped to his ankle and pulled out the small knife. He held this to his jugular, ready to give it one good jab. "Sorry, God, but I guess I wasn't a good choice after all!"

He saw a blur of motion, and something bowled into him, sending him spinning. He tried to catch himself, but his wrist was clamped in a vise grip hold. He slammed into a wall, and Tony's pretty face was inches away. "No you don't buster," she hissed. "You're not leaving me here all alone."

Her eyes were wide with alarm, and David thought that he could climb right into the inviting depths.

"Hold it," he cautioned, and closed his eyes a moment. When he opened them, she was still staring at him, still holding him immobile with surprising strength. "You can let me go now."

"Drop the knife," she ordered.

He let it go, and it floated away at about an inch a second. With one quick motion, she released him and snatched up the knife.

"God!" he called into the air. "God-damned it answer me!"

Silence.

He nodded to Tony and grinned. "I was just testing. I wanted to make sure he was really gone."

She nodded slowly herself, understanding now. "Good thinking. You don't believe him, do you? About thawing out more people."

"Nope. He didn't want to talk about it. Also, bringing Biosphere down out of orbit—that doesn't make sense, at least, not if you assume people are going to continue on from there. If he has any chance of winning this best-of-show cosmic competition, he obviously can't do it with . . ."

"Pets?" Tony suggested.

"I was thinking specimens. Anyway, he can't do it with prize contestants that have been given inside clues about Godly powers. Once he shows us how to bring Biosphere down, we're done. He'll have to get rid of us."

Tony looked truly scared. "What can we do? You can't escape from . . . God!"

"I have an idea. We won't escape—we'll just give a good tug back on the puppet strings."

ж ж ж

It was twenty minutes before God returned, and about time, David thought. His hands were getting sweaty, and holding death between his thumb and finger was beginning to unnerve him.

He could only guess how unnerved Tony was, strapped to him with their belts. They were back-to-back, so he couldn't see her face.

"Here you are," God's steady voice proclaimed. "What's going on? What you're doing is extremely dangerous."

"That's the idea," David confirmed.

For once in his life, he was happy for a design bug that he'd had to patch around months before, not having had time to implement a proper fix. Thus, it had been easy to pull the code Band-Aid so that the maneuvering rockets could be activated with the reflective coverings closed. The dead man's switch he held would fire the rockets located just beyond the bulkhead to which he and Tony were secured. The resulting cataclysm was hard to predict—at least for him, a mere human—but he was confident that, one way or another, both he and Tony would be dead once the dust settled. The fact that ARC-1 would also likely be destroyed was icing on the morbid cake.

"Tony," God admonished, letting something close to emotion color his voice for the first time, "I thought we had an agreement. What's this foolishness?"

"We just want some straight answers, that's all," she replied, giving one of the belts a tug to make sure it was tight.

"This is how you request information? By placing yourselves a sneeze away from obliteration?"

David took over. "It's the only leverage we have. We can't force you to tell us what we need to know, but we can make you really sorry if you don't. You need us."

"To complete the competition. That's true."

David felt a cold shiver at the implication: from God's point of view, it *was* just a competition. As far as they knew, he might have a happy God-family to go home to after spending some fun time with his Earth hobby.

"All we want is the truth," David reiterated.

"I always tell the truth."

"That may be, but there's a wide scattering of truths, and then there's the whole truth. Many people promised to tell this by placing their hand over your words—now it's your turn."

"That's quite impertinent coming from something I created."

"From what I understand, I'm as much an accident as anything planned by you."

"You know, this is exactly the behavior that's been causing me so much grief. So, what do you want to know?"

"Do you really plan on allowing us to gestate the humans?"

"I told you that I did."

"When?"

"As I explained, I plan on letting you activate the frozen human embryos last, after the rest of the animals."

"That sounds just too convenient. We carry through the whole show on the trust that humans will be thawed at the end. At that point our bargaining position won't be exactly compelling."

"You think you will need to bargain with your God?"

"My *God* just whacked the whole world! Yeah! I think a little caution is quite appropriate. So, when exactly will we thaw humans? Let's say we've just patted the last little bunny on its rump and set it hopping across the flowered meadow. Can the human embryos be thawed immediately after?"

"Approximately."

"What approximately? How can 'immediately after,' be approximated? Is 'approximately' five minutes or more like thirty minutes after the last bunny is set loose? How about a range?"

"Why are we quibbling?"

"Because you're stalling! This is not a difficult question!"

"It's complicated. You wouldn't understand."

"Look, God, you obviously know we're not going to like the answer, but here's the deal: you can tell us and we deal with the consequences, or I lift my finger off this button. In fact, I'm going to count to three: one—two—"

"My plan was that you could activate the human embryos ten seconds after the latter of you two expire."

Silence filled the cramped engineering hold like an evacuated beach sucked dry by a giant tsunami before crashing down.

"Did you just say that we would be allowed to thaw what's left of humanity *after* we are both dead?"

"Technically, yes."

"Why, you mealy-mouthed, cheating—"

"But you must understand. You two would have a good, full life. You will die of old age, happy and content. You will have everything your heart desires."

"And when we finally do die, that's the end of the human race. Kaput. Exterminated."

"I don't know why you have to couch everything so negatively."

"I guess we humans are just made of piss and vinegar. Okay, God-your-most-holy-highness, here's the real deal. Tony and I expected some kind of double-cross like this—"

"Now, hold on just a second—"

"Shut up and listen! The deal is that we will indeed bring Biosphere down to Borneo using your super-advanced science, and we will re-populate the Earth—the Earth that you yourself broke—and when we're done, you will help us lift biosphere back into orbit. From there we'll leave the Earth/moon system on our own and we promise to never come back. If we never have contact with Earth again, that should satisfy your Godly judges."

"But how can I trust *you?*"

David snorted. "You don't need to. You've already said you have domain over the whole solar system. If we ever come within a million miles of Earth, you can kill us . . . in some subtle way."

"Like," Tony suggested, "re-fold a few blood protein molecules into prions and we'd be dead in no time."

"Hmm, perhaps," God mulled. "I'll have to take some time to think this through—okay, I agree. With one stipulation, though."

"What's that."

"I can't take a chance by letting you hang around. You'll need to move away completely—off to another star system."

"Fat chance. Biosphere needs the sun for energy. Besides, Tony and I will die of old age before we hardly get out of the Solar System. Hatched human descendants wouldn't reach the nearest star for thousands of years, assuming Biosphere could even hold together that long."

"Oh, I can take care of that. I can show you how to fit Biosphere with an FTL drive—"

"FTL?" Tony asked.

"Faster Than Light," David explained. "So," he said into the air, "apparently once we bow out of the species-pageant competition, all manner of super-science opens up."

"What you call science, I call garage-shop. Look, this is wearing me out. I'm going to go and rest. Can I count on you to not blow yourselves up for a half-hour?"

"Maybe we need a . . . contract or something."

"Like a covenant? We've already tried that, remember? You'll just have to trust me. I'm actually happy with the deal. I can feel better about myself."

"A happy God is a happy world."

Silence.

"He must be gone," Tony said.

"Okay with me. I did just fine without him up to now; I'll be glad to be rid of him once we've re-seeded his mess and set off as the new Robinson family, minus Dr. Smith."

Tony reached down and undid the belt buckles. "You know, it's going to be strange activating the human embryos. We're going to be like parents with septuplets—octuplets—heck, what do you call a birth with a dozen babies?"

"Hmm, maybe we'll phase them—let each batch care for the next larger batch."

"See? Just like a real family. We'll be the proud grandparents."

Tony pulled off the last belt, and they drifted apart, but turned to face each other.

The only other human in the universe looked not at all like a grandmother to David. "You know, we could add a few home-grown spuds to the mix."

She eyed him skeptically, but then grinned. "The frozen embryos are carefully selected genetic icons of humanity. We'd just muck up the party."

"Sometimes a party needs a little mucking up to get off the ground."

She cocked her head seductively. "That's exactly the kind of rambunctious behavior God's trying to eliminate."

"And that's exactly why we'll be getting out of his hair. Give me rambunctiousness or give me death."

She pushed her foot against a pipe and shot off for the door. "Something tells me I may want to revisit those options someday."

Defense

Craig Bloss hadn't slept through the night in two decades, so he wasn't surprised when something woke him at 2:30 AM. Lying there in the dark, he at first took the crackling that he heard to be Miser getting into the bag of dog food he'd probably forgotten to put away. But he realized that the sound was not that of paper. He heard hissing and little pops, like the thirteen kilovolt transmission line that came down on the corner of his freshly plowed field, dancing and sparking, during the same spring storm that ripped off half the shingles from the silo.

Not taking the time to consider the improbability of this happening inside his old farmhouse, he leapt out of bed, nearly falling as he tripped over his shoes. Before he could turn on the light, the sound stopped. In the silence, he wasn't sure where it had come from. He'd thought it was right there in the house, but now he wasn't sure.

His heart stopped when a bang as loud as his twelve-gauge exploded nearby.

"Judas Priest!" he exclaimed.

The next instant a brilliant flare lit up the hallway outside the bedroom door, so bright that it hurt his night-adjusted eyes.

"Papa?"

It was his twelve year-old grandson who was staying with him in the guest room down the hall while his daughter took a honeymoon—her third—somewhere in the Caribbean.

"Come here, boy," he called, flipping on the bedroom light.

His charge didn't look very scared as he trotted in, his hair sticking up at odd angles. He still wore flannel kid-pajamas, and Craig had told himself that he would have to talk to the boy about that soon. He motioned for his grandson to get behind him while he jammed his feet into his slippers. "You stay here," he ordered and hurried down the hall and into the kitchen, turning on lights along the way. Everything seemed normal, although he thought he detected the smell of something scorched.

"I think it's in here, Papa!" Tod called from the living room.

"I thought I told you to stay—"

He was surprised to find Tod standing over a silver ball the size of a grape lying on the worn hardwood floor. Old Miser waddled in and sniffed at it suspiciously. The thing had done damage. It lay in a shallow depression, and the varnish was blistered for three feet all around.

"What the devil—is it some kind of meteor?" Craig whispered hoarsely, gazing up at the ceiling. But there was no hole, nothing to indicate it had come through the roof.

He squatted down to get a better look. He saw that the ball hadn't actually gouged the floor; it looked more like it had pressed into the floorboards for a few inches all around, creating a crater. The curved surface of the indented hardwood underneath the blistered varnish was perfectly smooth, as though someone had carefully pushed a bowling ball into soft clay.

"Well, I never . . ." he muttered.

"Maybe it came from, like, another dimension or something," Tod offered.

He looked up at the wide, excited eyes of his grandson. Tod lived in an apartment right next to a freeway and spent all his free time fooling around on the internet.

"Don't let your imagination run away with you, boy. There's gotta be an explanation, and somebody's gonna pay for the repairs, I can tell you that."

Hearing his own words, he stood up and peered out the window. All was dark. He would have seen anybody leaving along his quarter-mile lane to the highway.

He heard a zap, and Tod yelled, "Ouch!"

He turned to find the boy holding his pained foot.

"Wha'd ya do?"

"I just nudged it with my toe—or tried to. It wouldn't let me get close."

"Nonsense. Whatever it is, it's not alive."

Miser started barking at it, and Craig had to take him away and lock him in the basement.

Craig came back and squatted down again, reaching out to touch it. The next thing he knew, he was sitting on his ass realizing he'd been shocked. "Son of a bitch!"

He glanced over at his grandson. "Sorry. The damn thing *is* alive!"

"It seems to be, like, defending itself."

Craig was disinclined now to argue with the boy.

He got stiffly to his feet and contemplated the thing. It just sat there—no movement, no sound, totally passive . . . until you tried to get too close.

He went back to the bedroom to put on some clothes. It was funny, he thought, how even though Mary was gone now more than seven years, his instinctive reaction was still how upset she would be about the floor.

From the back of one of the kitchen drawers he found the grilling fork from the days when they'd host the family reunion picnics each summer. Although the tines were metal, the handle was wooden. That should do it.

He told the boy to get back as he squatted down and calculated his move. The fork looked wide enough to slide the tines along each side of the ball and lift it. He lay the fork flat on the floor and pushed it slowly forward.

"It's not going to like it," Tod warned.

"It's not supposed to," Craig replied without looking up.

As the tips came in along each side of the intruder, tiny little strings of blue light sizzled out to probe them, as though feeling what was approaching. Craig felt nothing through the wooden handle, though, so he slid the fork along some more.

Suddenly he jerked back as an ear-ringing bang stopped his heart for a second time. There was no smoke, no scorched smell; there had been no flash of light. But the fork was ruined, the tines bent apart. More than just bent apart, though. They were also curved, as though the same bowling ball that had dented the floor had now fallen from an airplane smack on the end of the fork. Where the bowling ball made contact, the metal of the tines was smooth and shiny.

"Son-of-a-bitch!" Craig exclaimed. Now he was getting mad. The damn thing came uninvited into *his* house, and now it acted like it owned the place.

He scrambled up, stormed past the wide-eyed boy, and made for the tool-shed. He came back with the long-handled sledgehammer.

"Hey, Papa!" Tod exclaimed. "Don't you think—"

"Stand back, boy—over there, near the door."

He lifted the hammer high, and let it fall. This time he was ready for the bang, and was actually surprised that the hammer didn't jolt and sting his hands when the mini-explosion rattled the windows and set his ears ringing. In fact, it felt as though it had given way, as if he'd just crushed a stone. Except that now the sledgehammer was also ruined—the flat side of the head splayed out and carved in the same concave dent. He could see his own distorted face in the smooth inside surface.

More exasperating, the dent in the floor was now about twice as big.

"You—little—bastard," he breathed as he swung the ruined hammer like a golf club. Once again the sphere took him by surprise by doing nothing, passively allowing itself be knocked to roll across the floor, bounce off the far wall, and come to rest against the throw rug.

"Well," Craig uttered puzzled, but satisfied with his little success. "That's better. Open the front door, boy."

Mary liked to play miniature golf at the county fair, and she was good—beat him every time. He didn't have to be very good to win this one, though. He got as many swings as he liked. The ball was now just a ball. It rolled and bounced its way in turns out of the living room, through the front entrance where he kept his boots and coats, and out and down the steps into the black night. He wondered if maybe it was out of juice.

He decided he wasn't comfortable just leaving it out there in the yard, though. Even though its batteries seemed to be shot, it had packed a powerful punch. It was like leaving a wounded rattlesnake or stick of dynamite out there. He flipped on the outside floodlight and followed it out.

"Maybe we should call the FBI," Tod said from the doorway. "Or maybe some scientists."

Where do you find a scientist, Craig wondered as he scanned the dew-covered grass. The Yellow Pages? "I'll call the college in the morning," he replied.

It was just a two-year community college, but they must have somebody there that could take the damn thing off his hands.

Ah, there it was. It wasn't easy to see. The surface was dull, not like the imprint it left behind when it punched outward. He looked around. The tool-shed door was still open. It seemed as good a place as any. In three swings he putted the ball inside. He heard it rattle against the cowling of the lawn tractor and bounce off a shovel, and he swung the door closed and flipped the hasp over the ring-latch. He didn't bother to dig out a padlock; if somebody wanted to steal the destructive little devil, they were welcome to it. Good riddance.

"Back to bed, boy," he told his grandson. "Excitement's done for the night."

Craig knew he wouldn't sleep, but the boy needed the discipline of routine. Three in the morning was a time to be in bed.

Ж Ж Ж

The blast sounded like the sonic booms the F-105s made flying low above the treetops in Vietnam. Rocketing along faster than sound, they'd suddenly appear out of nowhere and be gone by the time the shock wave smacked into him. It nearly knocked him off his feet then, and it nearly shook him out of bed now.

The first light of dawn filled the room with a gray flatness, but was replaced by a momentary burst of sunlight as he stumbled to a window. The brilliant flash ended as abruptly as it had appeared, and by the time he peered out into the yard, the only light was from the flames growing to engulf the termite-riddled tool-shed even as he watched. A billowing fireball, the gas from the tractor's tank, as big as the shed itself rose slowly into the air like the soul of the old building, angry that it had been released without proper ceremony.

The dry, porous wood burned like kindling, and the little structure he'd known all his life was gone, collapsing in on itself, even before Tod ran in yelling hysterically. In the few moments he had to observe its death throes, though, Craig could see that the roof had been blown off, and the walls seemed to bow outward, as though inflated by the heat from within.

"It's the alien, isn't it Papa! It's the alien!" his grandson shouted.

"What are you talking about, boy?" he growled as he yanked on his pants for the second time.

"The thing from another dimension! It must be an alien!"

"Nonsense," Craig growled.

But as he stormed down the hall and out through the kitchen door, he warned himself that the crazy episode in the middle of the night hadn't been a dream. He didn't doubt that the damn ball was behind this. He was just glad he hadn't let the miserable thing remain inside the house. Lord, what if he hadn't been able to get to Tod in time—but there was no sense worrying himself over that. It hadn't happened.

At least, he consoled himself, it looked like the little bastard ball had done itself in, cremated by its own mischievous hands.

Craig stopped short.

There was something inside the burning pile of rotting lumber. It became more visible by the second as the remnant flaming planks disintegrated and fell away. It was about the size of his grandson's soccer ball, and the curved surface reflected the engulfing flames dully, almost reluctantly.

"Good Lord!" he cried.

It was the damn abominable ball, but . . . bigger—ten times as big.

"It's protecting itself," Tod said next to him.

Craig looked down at his grandson, relieved again that he'd moved the ball outside. He didn't reply to the boy, but just looked back to the dying fire, waiting to get closer to inspect this next development.

"The first one was a scout," Tod declared.

"What are you babbling about, boy?"

His grandson hesitated, studying his toe as it dug at the grass. He shrugged. "Maybe they sent the first one through to check things out. This one followed."

"The aliens."

"Right."

"From another dimension."

"Yeah."

He wasn't going to argue with the boy.

"You stay here," he ordered. "Don't move a muscle."

The heat was still intense, but he was able to get close enough now to pick up a rake handle that had blown free and poke past the glowing embers at the new ball. He wasn't surprised when blue dancing fingers arced to the handle tip, larger and fiercer that before. He *was* surprised, though, that he now felt a shock, sharp teeth nipping cruelly at his palm. The voltage had to be huge for that to happen.

Anger welled up again and he gave the pumpkin-sized sphere a good shove with the handle. A sharp bang marked the disintegration of its tip, the wood fibers peeled apart like a banana skin, but he'd managed to roll the ball a little. It came to rest at the edge of shed's foundation, teetered a moment, then fell off the six-inch ledge and rolled another dozen feet across the dirt to the top of the bank, where it continued down the slight incline and finally stopped behind the barn.

From behind him came a low, guttural growl. He'd forgotten about Miser. "Down, boy! Heel!"

The old dog was hard of hearing, but probably wouldn't have listened anyway. Craig wouldn't have guessed the old mutt could move so fast, right past him as he grabbed at his collar. He was caught off guard, though, and before he could recover and go after his ailing companion, a sizzling ZAP! announced the futility.

"Miser!" Tod cried, starting for the dog, and Craig had to lunge to stop him.

"You stay right here, boy. Don't move! You hear me? Not a goddamn finger!"

Craig looked at his old friend and cursed silently. The dog lay there, pitifully crumpled. At least he went down fighting.

Craig found a blackened limb trimmer from the shed's wreckage and used it to pull Miser back by his collar. The alien ball let its victim go without a peep. Craig saw that the dog's eyes had burst open as though the fluid inside had boiled. He carried the limp body down the bank, out of Tod's view. He'd bury Miser later.

He then got the hose and, keeping a healthy distance from the unwelcome visitor, sprayed down the smoldering embers around the farthest corner. He wanted to get a look inside.

Anything made of wood had been burned to cinders, but the few metal-handled tools were bent into a curve. They'd also been flattened, as though a giant had grabbed them at both ends and squashed them around a wrecking ball. It was the bowling ball signature of the living room floor, only on a ten-fold larger scale.

His yard tractor was the most fascinating. He hardly recognized it. From one side, he could make out the bent and twisted surrealistic shapes of an air-cleaner cover here, a wheel hub there, and what must have been part of the air-cooling fins of the engine block. From the other side, though, everything—metal, plastic, rubber—had been smeared together into a smooth uninterrupted surface. He peered at the oddly intriguing piece of modern-art from various angles, and was almost gratified to see that the overall surface was perfectly concave. The wrecking ball had been busy. He gingerly slid his finger along the surface. Even though his touch traversed dark plastic, shiny metal, and even the end of a clipped off piece of wire, he could discern no boundaries. It was as if the whole remains of the tractor were one continuous medium.

"It pushed everything away when it arrived," Tod said behind him.

Craig glanced around, ready to order his grandson back, but changed his mind. The boy wasn't scared, just fascinated by the unearthly phenomena. Sort of took after his old Papa.

"Think so, huh?" Craig murmured, turning back to his inspection.

Pushed everything away. Well, that's what an explosion does, Craig thought.

Wait a second.

Just saying the word in his mind sounded wrong. It wasn't an explosion that had done this. He played back events. Both times he'd been wakened by a loud noise—a noise that *sounded* like an explosion. But the flash of light, although coming right on the heels of the bang, wasn't simultaneous. It came after the sound. If anything, the light should arrive before the sound.

And both times, the sound wasn't really like an explosion. It was more like air and wood and metal being pushed back, out of the way. Really, really fast. Faster than . . . faster than sound, maybe.

What could do that? A force field? He didn't even know what a force field was. Hell, he probably wouldn't understand how it had done this if he *knew* what it was.

He stood up and looked at his grandson. The boy gazed back with eyes wide with sheer wonder. Craig put his hand on his grandson's shoulder and led him around to the front yard, where they both sat in the rickety and peeling Adirondack chairs that Mary had kept so nice by stripping and painting every other year. That woman had thrown nothing away.

"You think that first little ball was just an advance scout—that what you said?" Craig asked.

He hadn't meant for it to sound so . . . challenging. Tod looked at him cautiously. Craig realized that the boy was probably used to being constantly corrected and reprimanded by his mother. Hell, by him too.

He tried again, smiling this time.

"If the first ball was the scout, what do you think this one is?"

His grandson shrugged. The boy still wasn't sure what to make of this interrogation.

Craig let out an exaggerated sigh and shook his head. He chuckled and said, "Ever see anything like this on TV?"

Tod shook his head slowly, tentatively. "I read stuff, though."

This was more like it. "Science fiction?"

His grandson nodded, watching to see if that was a bad thing.

Craig grinned. "Looks like we're right smack in the middle of a science fiction story, eh?"

Tod grinned back and his nod was enthusiastic.

"So," Craig suggested, "you think there's little aliens inside this ball?"

His grandson considered a moment and shook his head. "This is just the next scout."

"The *next* one?"

"Uh-huh. They could only get a little one through at first, and that one . . . sort of pulled this next one through—"

"Through what?"

"The edges of the different dimensions."

"Kind of like a calf being born. Except each calf immediately gives birth to another one—ten times bigger."

Tod nodded with vigor.

Craig sat back in the low, reclining chair and contemplated his grandson. "So this one will pull the next one through—one even bigger. One maybe big enough to hold the actual aliens."

"Sure."

He knew they could only go so far with imagination and wild hypothesis, but he hated to dampen the roll they were on. "And you think these scouts—these probes—are just defending themselves."

"Well, sure. Wouldn't you?"

Indeed. Indeed.

ж ж ж

The flashes of light had come after the booms. He was sure of this, and he kept telling himself so to make sure that he stayed sure.

The fact was important.

At the expense of two brooms, an old cow prod, and three nasty shocks, he'd managed to nudge the ball into the barn. Tod sat on the floor at a safe distance, carefully measuring pennies into feed sacks and then tying them with pieces of baling twine, both of which lay around in scattered abundance. Craig had ferried over three hundred pounds of Mary's pennies from the cellar in his wheelbarrow. She'd started decades ago by throwing all the spare change into a jar. She'd said it was vacation money. It didn't take long for her to pare that back to just the pennies, but eventually the jar was full, and she moved up to a bucket, and finally just took them down and tossed them into the coal bin next to the new oil heater. He'd named the dog as a little joke on her. As he hauled them to Tod's little bagging factory, he calculated that there must be over five-hundred dollars worth—a vacation never spent.

With the pennies all transferred, Craig was now hanging the penny bags from the rafters and hay loft planks. He wasn't sure how far away to place them, but based on the two push-aways they'd already seen, he was guessing that if the next ball was, say, ten feet in diameter, then the push-away distance might be perhaps fifty or a hundred feet from that. It was all guesswork, but if his plan was right, it wouldn't much matter as long as the bags weren't outside the limit. He guessed that the more important point was to get them spread evenly. To that effect, he carried some down to the lower level, laying them in a circle underneath the ball waiting patiently just above.

If his plan was *not* correct, well, he just hoped the aliens didn't walk out carrying laser handguns.

"How about here, Papa?" Tod asked as Craig climbed back up the ladder to the main level.

His grandson was holding a bag in one hand and reaching up with the other to throw the twine over a rafter. He'd filled all the bags, and now wanted to help some more. "Listen, boy, I want you to—"

Craig was going to tell him to move outside of the barn. He had no way to know when the next phase would come though, but if the time span was the same as between the first two, it could be imminent. But as his grandson turned resignedly to receive an order, Craig changed his mind. "No, that spot is just fine. Fills a big gap right there. Good work."

Ten minutes later, they had hung all the bags and retired to the house. They sat looking out the kitchen window at first, but Craig got nervous, and they moved to the basement, where Tod now stood on a chair peering through the dirty window.

"Do you think it will work, Papa?"

"If not, we may all have to learn how to speak alien."

"You think they're just defending themselves—with the push-away and the fire?"

"Don't know. Maybe they're coming in blind, and just want to make sure nothing's dangerous nearby."

His grandson chewed his lip a moment. "What if . . ."

"Yeah?"

"Well, what if they aren't really, like, dangerous."

"Fair question. Well, first off, they did come in sort of swinging. They killed old Miser, after all. I think they would have killed us just as quickly if they had the chance."

"But these first ones might be only unmanned probes. They wouldn't really know what they're doing."

"Yeah, well somebody at the other end still had to design them. Listen, you know about the European settlers and the trouble they had with the Indians, right?"

"You mean that we're like the Europeans, and the aliens are Indians?"

"Uh, actually the other way around. If the Indians were smarter, or maybe just not so accommodating, they would have massacred every European that set foot on their land."

"You really believe that?"

"The Indians might have been better off. Our ancestors wouldn't have been real happy about it. But, maybe we wouldn't have been so quick to give 'em such a raw deal."

"I see . . ." Tod mulled. He shrugged. It is what it is. "You said you wished Gramma was here to see how she maybe was going to save our lives with her pain-in-the-ass hoard of pennies."

"That I did, although you can forget you heard that particular way of puttin' it. You remember your Gramma?"

"Kind of. I remember sitting at the table and she wouldn't let me get up until I ate all my scrambled eggs."

Craig chuckled. "That would be her. She probably told you that the hen had worked real hard to make the egg; the least you could do was swallow it."

They gazed together at the barn, every cracked plank and stone etched so deeply into Craig's head, he thought he could draw it down to the last detail with his back turned.

"You said you'd tell me later why we used pennies," Tod reminded him.

"They're copper. I remember from *my* school days that copper was the first metal the cavemen started to use. One reason was because it could be hammered and bent into shape. It's mail-able"

"I think you mean malleable."

He looked at his grandson who continued to gaze out the window. Maybe living in an apartment next to a freeway and spending his time fiddling around with computers didn't hurt so much after all.

Tod heard it first and snapped his head around and their eyes met. To Craig, it sounded like the very Earth was tearing apart at the seams. It was the snap-crackle-and-pop of the night before, only volcano-sized. It was the sound of pure, massive energy.

He felt the boom first in his soles as the massive push-away slammed into the earth under the barn. He struggled to stay on his feet amidst the earthquake. He clutched the window sill and stared out. The tin roof bulged upward from the shock wave. Planks flew from the sides, somersaulting away. *Come on!* he prayed. *Blast away with that devil light.* If it took too long, the copper within the penny bags, stretched and pulled into perfect spherical mirrors by their own push-away, would tumble away, losing the focus on the new emerging ball.

As he had carried Miser down the bank, he'd flashed back to Vietnam, and how American fighters were brought down by Vietcong with their own captured shoulder-fired Redeye SAMs. What was his Redeye SAM? Weapon designers, human or alien, would probably always assume they were fighting technologies as sophisticated as their own. Perhaps it was a kind of war hubris. They would use defensive weapons that could best their own technology. The Vietcong had used American SAMs against the US Airforce; he'd let the aliens burn under their own devil light.

But only if they *didn't wait too long!* The stretched copper pennies would hover as a perfect mirror for only a fleeting moment.

Perhaps it was instinct, or maybe a part of his brain that worked faster than the conscious gears, but before he realized he'd even done it, Craig grabbed Tod and pulled him away from the window, shielding his grandson with his body as the glass exploded inward, and the concussion sent them sprawling to the dirt floor.

They lay there and listened as pieces of the barn rained down on the house. After a minute there was only silence, broken only by the distant sound of the neighbor's dog barking hysterically.

Outside, the barn was gone. Even the foundation was smashed and scattered. He never imagined that he'd ever look at his obliterated barn and think that it was the best thing he'd ever laid eyes on.

They poked around the debris, but could find no trace of the second ball, or anything that looked like it might have been of alien manufacture. Tod put forth the theory that maybe the aliens had realized in time what was happening and pulled back to their own dimension. Craig wasn't about to question the boy about what aliens might do, not anymore. He only hoped the bastards got singed enough to stay on their own side.

A morose siren wailed to life. The volunteer crew would be here in ten minutes. He'd have that much time to think of some plausible reason why his barn had spontaneously disintegrated.

In the meantime, he was going to have a beer. He put his arm around Tod and they walked towards the house.

"Do you like wearing those flannel pajamas?" he asked.

His grandson thought a moment and shook his head.

"Tell you what, boy—you can wear a pair of mine for now, and I'll talk to your mom when she gets back."

"Okay . . . and, Papa?"

"Yep?"

"Could you call me by my name?"

Craig stopped. He'd never considered that his grandson might not like being called just "boy." He chuckled. He sounded like Tarzan.

"You got it, Tod" he said, holding out his hand.

His grandson paused just a moment before reaching out to return the grasp firmly.

The Shoes of Moses

Moses sat at the edge of the Red Sea with his elbows on his knees, and his chin cupped in his hands.

"I hate to rush you, Mose," said his brother, Aaron, "but Pharaoh's army has crossed the far dunes. They're maybe an hour away."

"Then don't," the founder of Israel replied, staring out over the choppy waters.

Yahweh hadn't been specific when he had told him at the burning bush that he was to be granted the power of miracles in order to free his people from Egypt. Moses had learned that this charter wasn't cart blanche. For example, although he had managed to bring a plague of locusts down on the Pharaoh's head, and turn the Nile to blood—both pretty impressive in Moses' eyes—he wasn't able to get rid of the eczema on his ankles, no matter how impressively he commanded it. It was as though God had a bag of certain miracles he held out to Moses, and it was his task to try and grab the right one for the right job. Only, he didn't even know what was in the bag when he reached blindly in.

Moses had a sense that this was one of those miracle times. The Egyptian army was hot on their trail, the Red Sea stretched out before them, and there wasn't a boat in sight. Should he reach into the bag and try to pull out a dozen boats? Somehow, based on the previous miracles, he guessed that Yahweh was counting on something more impressive. After all, how miraculous would it sound centuries later that Moses had led his people to safety in . . . boats? Maybe if they were boats made of ice gliding over a sea of burning coals. But, no. The theatre would seem too fabricated. People might not believe it thousands of years down the road.

No, Moses guessed that Yahweh had something simple, yet awe-inspiring in mind. Maybe they would just walk across, walk right over the top of the water. He quickly rejected that as well. It sounded fine at first: "He could walk on *water!*" But then the image of his people seen from a distance, shuffling along on the horizon, dropping things, wandering off to the side to pee, seemed altogether ordinary. No, it just wasn't impressive enough. It might work great for a man alone ... but Moses decided to leave that for someone else.

On the other hand, if they were going to walk across ... maybe they needed something else big enough to take the attention off of them. And then it hit him. Of course! They wouldn't walk *on* the water—the sea would make way *for* them!

Moses was sweating by now. This was so stressful. Each time one of these miracle events came along, he wondered if he was going to figure it out in time. He always worried that maybe this was the one; he'd reach in the bag, and it would be empty.

He stood up and stretched out his arms, holding his trusty cane in his fist like an upturned sword. "Lord, the one true God!" he cried as the wind picked up and flogged his long beard dramatically. "Part these waters so that my people can pass to safety!"

On the other hand, there was no greater thrill than when he did figure it out and commanded something stupendous. The ground shook, and a widening depression formed in the water before him.

Ж Ж Ж

It stunk. He hadn't anticipated that. They were only a couple of hundred yards from the shore, and already it was almost unbearable. He never would have guessed that the bottom of a sea would smell so bad. It reeked of fish and slime and rotting algae. Worse, they had to wade through it. The farther they got from the shore, the deeper the stinking muck became. It was already up to their knees. With each step, they had to struggle to pull their foot back out, and when it did come, there was a sickening sucking sound, and more often than not, the sandal stayed behind. Then they had to balance on one foot and try to yank it out without falling on their back into the goo.

All around him the people of Israel muttered and cursed with every hard won stride. They didn't even notice the massive walls of water towering above them on both sides any more. By Moses' calculation, Pharaoh's army would be on top of them in less than a half hour. They would be caught helpless, struggling to pull a sandal from the mud while a soldier on horseback ran a spear through them like they were shish kebab. Something had to be done, but he had the clear feeling that the miracle bag was indeed now empty.

ж ж ж

The Egyptian general paused his army at the shore. He'd had about enough of this Yahweh's miracles. He would gladly take on any opposing army on a level playing field, but it just wasn't fair when the rules of the game could change at any moment. And now, here in front of him, yet another miraculous sight: a tremendous canyon of water stretching away as far as his eyes could see. He somehow knew that he was playing the fool, but there for everyone to see were the Hebrew's footprints leading into the mud. He really didn't have any choice.

Fifty yards from shore he knew that this was not as easy as it had looked. Of course. The mud was getting thicker, and the horses were slowing down. And, the stink! Whew! But, as long as the footprints of the fugitives continued on before them, he had to follow.

Fifteen minutes later they came to a stop once more. The holes in the mud made by struggling legs suddenly disappeared! It was as though each of the limbs' owners had simply vanished.

Not exactly. The footprints hadn't disappeared completely. He could see that, leading away from each last hole, was a line of circular imprints perhaps half a cubit across. He didn't stop to contemplate this; fate awaited. He raised his arm and led his men on through the sucking muck.

Hours later, far from sight of the Egyptian shore, the general heard a rumble. He wasn't really surprised, and he wasn't really angry. He understood that they were simply pawns in the hands of this spectacle-loving Yahweh.

ж ж ж

On the far shore of the Red Sea, in the land of Sinai, Moses sat with his people and watched the walls of water crash back together. He had done it again. He felt overwhelming relief wash through him, and decided that they would break out the wine skins that night. He needed the deep sleep of a good intoxication.

The waters of the Red Sea settled, and the people of Israel continued untying the cooking pans from their feet.

Aaron sat down next to Moses. "That was brilliant, Mose. I suppose you had a vision from God that wearing the pans would let us walk over the mud?"

Moses gave him a reproving look. "I can take credit for at least one miracle."

He held up the pot he'd just taken off. "In a pinch," he said, "you sometimes have to think outside the bag."

The Full Story

You are a lilly-ass," Briantte hissed before slamming the door of the Escalade SUV in his face.

"I think you mean lilly-livered," Dave replied quietly to the fishtailing rear, as spinning tires threw African sand across his T-shirt and shorts.

"More like a panzy-ass," McCabe huffed next to him. "Why'd you let her go?"

Dave looked at the man who was the root of the problem. Dumpy and balding, he looked more like a siding salesman than a CIA operative as Briantte maintained. "What was I supposed to do? Tie her up?"

"You're the news producer," the unwelcome man challenged. "Aren't you supposed to be the boss on assignments?"

"You've got to be joking. Briantte's ten million worshiping viewers collectively declare that she can do whatever she wants. Ratings are ad revenue, and ad revenue rules."

The truth was that, although he never verbalized it, Dave felt more like a road manager than a news producer.

McCabe watched him dispassionately. He never got excited, but never seemed to relax either. It was as though he was expecting something to happen at any moment, something you weren't aware of.

After a moment, McCabe scowled. "It's your job. It's not complicated."

Dave felt the bile rising. "My job," he repeated. "Okay, let's talk about jobs. What exactly is your job here?" He yanked the memo from his back pocket, tearing it in his rush of anger. "Let's see—what does it say? Hmm, you're supposed to be my co-producer." He jammed the paper back in his pocket, feeling it rip even more. "Well, co-producer, what would you have done?"

McCabe smiled ever so slightly, seeming to be pleased that he'd gotten a reaction. "I would have simply ordered her to get out of the car and go through with the interview she came six thousand miles to do, instead of acting like a spoiled kid."

"Ha! You—*you* would have ordered her? It's because of *you* that she left . . . wait a second, did you say spoiled kid?"

His co-producer of twelve hours lifted one eyebrow in surprise at his obvious over-reaction. "Okay. How about irresponsible behavior? Or failing of integrity. Is that less offensive? Does that suit your panzy-ass sensibility better?"

Dave felt his face grow even hotter under the sub-tropical desert sun. "What the *hell* do you know about integrity? She left because she *has* integrity! When the government thinks it can just waltz in and use journalists as—"

McCabe had stepped towards him. His face still bore the same bland casual indifference, but the eyes bore through him like diamond-tipped drill bits. "Let's not get carried away," he urged. His voice was calm, almost soothing, but the hand that grasped Dave's elbow was an iron claw.

He shook it off, and the faux co-producer held on a bare fraction of a second before releasing him—just long enough to demonstrate that he was in control. The young rebel fighters—teenage boys, really, whose only uniform consisted of varying styles of long, khaki pants and a blue ribbon tied around their upper arms—had gone quiet and sat around in the shade watching them. They didn't understand English, but recognized an argument when they saw one.

At that moment, Dave knew that it was true. Briantte was right. In his frustration, he'd been ranting whatever nonsense came into his head, but he had hit too close to home. Hell, based on McCabe's reaction, he'd hit the bullseye.

The planted agent studied him a moment as if sizing him up. "You'll do the interview."

"What are you talking about? I'm not a journalist."

"You don't need to be. You made up the script questions yourself. You just read them off and record Erasto's answers."

"Erasto only agreed to the interview because he trusts Briantte."

McCabe shook his head as though disgusted with Dave's whining. "It won't hurt to try."

Erasto, the rebel leader, was portrayed as a terrorist by the conservative news media, following the lead of the Administration. It had been Briantte's coverage of the alleged abuses by the Abujan national government that had attracted the favor of the charismatic Muslim rebel. Dave doubted that Erasto would be willing to continue without her.

In fact, he was.

The leader's aide explained that his boss was committed to using any opportunity available to expose the atrocities routinely inflicted by the Abujan army.

Dave opened the van to haul out the video equipment, but McCabe told him not to bother, that just an audio recording would do.

"Who's the producer here?" Dave asked.

"So, produce. Without Briantte, though, there's really no point in bothering with video recording."

This wasn't true. Media news thrived on images. He reached in to grab a bundle of tripods, and the iron grip once again caught his elbow. "I think the audio will do just fine," McCabe's deadly calm voice assured.

Dave tried to shake him off, but this time the agent held tight.

"Don't fuck with me," McCabe warned quietly, his voice now a low growl.

With his left hand, Dave peeled the iron fingers from his arm.

"Fine," he replied without bothering to contain the volume. "Let's get this over with and get the hell out of here so I can file a complaint."

That was bullshit, and he knew it. Ever since the Long Beach dirty bomb, Homeland Security had effectively wielded marshal law. Trying to lodge a complaint would simply get him on the

Noncooperatives List, the modern-day version of the McCarthy commie roll-call.

Inside the spare stone and mortar building—the all-purpose courthouse, post-office, and police station for this far-flung province, and the only permanent structure in the village—teenage soldiers searched them. Since all Dave brought was his pocket audio recorder, the process was over in seconds. They were then led into a small room outfitted with just a table and wooden chairs to wait for Erasto, but before they got settled, McCabe announced that he'd better make a bathroom run before they got started. He slung one arm casually over Dave's shoulder and said quietly into his ear, "I'll meet you at the van."

Dave looked at him in surprise, and his ad-hoc co-producer added, "You'll know what I'm talking about," before walking out.

He didn't have time to wonder what shenanigans the agent was up to, for the rebel leader strode in, followed by two senior soldiers who took up positions on each side of the door. A nervous young woman peeked through the door and entered, introducing herself with a British flavored accent as the translator. Erasto, appearing every bit as handsome and confident as his reputation promised, pulled a chair into the corner next to the window, a position safe from sniper shots. The army lieutenant-turned-adversary folded his arms across his chest and nodded at them to proceed.

Dave glanced across his script sheet. How different the questions looked when it was him doing the asking. For a brief moment, he wondered if he could deliver them with the same earnest enthusiasm as Briantte did, as though she was thinking them up herself as the interview progressed. But he reminded himself that there was no camera watching, and in any case, whatever emotional nuance he managed would be diluted or even lost through the translation anyway.

As it turned out, he could have thrown the script away. Erasto had his own agenda, and no matter what Dave asked, each answer twisted around back to the abuses of the national army. At one point the leader thanked Dave for his courage, since it was obvious to the whole world that the US openly supported Abujan's President, even though the elections had been a blatant scam—declared so, in fact, by the monitoring NGO. The fact that

Abujan served as a potentially valuable staging area in the covert war against the Chinese-backed Somalis was lost on nobody, apparently, except the American network media.

At one point, as Dave waited for the translation of some impassioned and incomprehensible point, he heard a buzzing sound, and a moment later, a large insect flew through the window. It looked like a fat dragonfly, and he wondered idly as he waited for Erasto to finish how it survived in the Danakil desert. He remembered vaguely that they laid their eggs in ponds. The handsome leader glanced at the bug and gave it an annoyed swipe with his hand, but the winged beast deftly swerved and rose out of reach.

The two guards, watching alertly from their positions at the door, frowned at the exotic intruder as it maneuvered above and behind Erasto's head. Dave imagined that they were considering what to do about the pest. Perhaps rush forward and start swatting at it with the tips of their rifles? Maybe lift the weapons and begin taking potshots all around their leader?

It was these idle thoughts that sparked the connection in Dave's head. McCabe had insisted that they go forward with the interview, at the same time refusing to even consider video recording. The faux co-producer worked for an agency not noted for a high regard for human lives, an agency of a government that was looking to curry favor from the Abujan president. And finally, with an enigmatic instruction, he'd excused himself to go to the bathroom, but, importantly, was not in the room now.

Nobody had ever thought it odd that Clark Kent and Superman, or Peter Parker and Spiderman were never seen together.

Shit!

The hovering interloper had settled in behind Erasto's head where the rebel leader couldn't easily swipe at it. The blur of artificial wings buzzed with a tone that seemed to have suddenly turned ominous, as though the incredible tiny machine was gathering strength.

"Look out!" Dave shouted, jumping to his feet.

Instantly, the guards sprang forward, one grabbing his elbows and yanking them painfully behind his back, the other stabbing the tip of his rifle against his cheek.

As Dave watched horrified, the tiniest of glints shot from the assassin drone, just where its mouth would have been were it a real insect.

But Erasto had also reacted to Dave's shout, and started to stand up. The needle had been aimed to strike at the rebel's scalp or bare neck, but disappeared behind him. The leader wore a flak jacket, and this, impenetrable to both bullets and tiny needles, saved his life.

The miniature drone hovered for an eternal second before zipping out the window and away.

Neither Erasto nor his personal guards understood how close death had flirted.

Chaos swirled through the room a few minutes as the rattled translator stammered questions and responses back and forth. Dave suddenly found himself in the excruciating dilemma whereby he had to adequately explain his outburst without ratting out his planted co-producer. Unable to think of anything else, he explained that he thought the dragonfly was a rare poisonous insect he'd read about, and then realized that maybe he'd hit a little too close to home. Erasto didn't seem to be buying it, though. The insurgent watched Dave's face, and he had the distinct impression that the rebel leader was reading his false sincerity even though he couldn't understand the actual words.

Dave was saved by the very man for whom he was providing cover. Shouting, interrupted by gunshots, broke up their interrogation, and against the protests of his guards, Erasto strode out to see what was happening. After a moment of uncertainty, they followed their leader, dragging Dave along.

Dave gasped and froze when he saw the result of the commotion, causing his escort guard to jerk his arm painfully. McCabe lay on the ground surrounded by teenage soldiers all pointing their rifles at his chest, which blossomed in red, the blood spreading across his shirt even as Dave watched. The sight was terrifying, almost unreal in the degree of extreme violence. He had seen it enacted so many times in movies that bullets and blood had come to be no less abstract than laser pistols and matter transporters.

This was real blood, however. And McCabe was really dead.

The youthful rebel soldiers looked on casually. They had seen and drawn enough blood in their short lives that McCabe's last moments of life were of no more consequence than a chicken they might slaughter for supper.

Erasto was not casual. The man dead on the ground was not an inconsequential Abujan soldier, but, he believed, an American news representative. He shouted questions, breaking the languid calm of the young fighters who slowly realized that it was them he was angry with, not the uncooperative foreigner they'd brought down. Erasto picked up a satchel lying next to McCabe, a bag the agent had been carrying ever since he joined the news team. He tore it open and pulled out a flat bundle of stiff cloth, which unfolded into what looked like Batman's mask, except where the holes for eyes would have been were bulging domes. Dropping the bizarre mask to the ground, he extracted a small metal box inset with two push-buttons and a hole half an inch across. He looked at Dave.

"He wants to know what it is," the translator said. She must have followed on behind them, and her voice quavered with emotion.

Dave shook his head slowly. "I have no idea."

He heard his own words, and they sounded as though he was listening to a recording played back.

Erasto barked questions to his boy-soldiers and then turned again to the translator, taking a deep breath before asking a question of her with a forced calm.

"Why was your colleague running away?" she conveyed. "He wouldn't stop when commanded to do so."

Dave looked at the lifeless face of McCabe. *Because he had just tried to kill you*, Dave thought. He didn't say this. Instead he reminded them that neither of them spoke their language, and his colleague wouldn't have understood what the young fighters were shouting.

When told this, Erasto stood for a few moments in scowled thought, clearly debating a most unwelcome development. Finally, he put the mysterious box back into the satchel, followed by the

Batman mask, from which he wiped off the dust onto his pants first, and then handed the bag to Dave.

"He says he is very sorry," the translator said. "It must have been a misunderstanding. Sad and unjust things happen in war all the time. You came to see it, and now you have experienced it."

That was the last Erasto talked to Dave. The insurgent leader strode off, and not sure how else to handle the situation, Dave began shuffling equipment around in the van to make room for McCabe's body.

And that's why the small handheld video camera happened to be within reach when the Abujan army attacked. Gunfire erupted some hundreds of yards away and quickly moved towards the small village. The two dozen teenage fighters retreated through the scattered trees before an entire company of over a hundred uniformed soldiers, but stood their ground once they reached the settlement, firing from the cover of the huts while Erasto gathered his belongings and tossed them into the back of his jeep. As soon as their leader sped away, the teenage fighters seemed to melt into the ground. The Abujan soldiers, finding that their gunfire was no longer being returned, moved in cautiously.

Dave had filmed the battle using the van for protection. He'd caught two Abujan soldiers fall and the capture of one of the young fighters. The boy had taken a bullet in his knee, and although two of his comrades tried to drag him along with them, the advancing army company had forced them to leave the bleeding youth. The fighting was now over, but he continued to film the soldiers as they searched the village for stragglers and booby traps. Had he been satisfied to put away the camera sooner, he probably would have hung on to the digital images, but he didn't see the Abujan captain come striding in once the area was secure, and so closed up the camera and tucked it away out of sight too late.

The squat, no-nonsense officer came over and introduced himself in slow, careful English. He explained that he had been sent to save the Americans who were reported kidnapped, and was glad that they had arrived in time. When Dave protested that they had come of their own free will and were not being restrained at all, the Abujan captain peered into the dark interior at McCabe's corpse and turned to him with furrowed brow. "Are you telling me you killed this man yourself?" he asked in a threatening tone.

"No!" Dave exclaimed. "Of course not. They shot him . . . but it was an accident—a miscommunication."

The captain eyed him. "You know, rebel sympathizers are punished as though they are rebels themselves."

"I'm not sympathizing with anybody. I came to get an objective story. Look," he urged, pulling the official transcripts from his back pocket, "we cleared this with the Abujan State Department before we left."

He was speaking for himself. McCabe's agenda was his own, and he wasn't talking.

The captain gave the papers a mere glance, hardly taking enough time to even see what they were. "I am a soldier, not a bureaucrat," he declared, but handed them back, apparently satisfied. He then reached in and pulled out the video camera that Dave had tried to hide. "You won't be needing this."

"Hey!" Dave cried as his rescuer walked away shouting orders. "You can't just take that!"

Evidently he could.

The captain assigned one of his men to drive the van, and Dave sat in the passenger seat. The back doors suddenly opened, and soldiers pushed the young wounded rebel in on top of McCabe. The boy moaned at the pain, but otherwise was quiet, perhaps taking his cue from the dead CIA agent.

Before they took off, the captain walked up carrying McCabe's satchel. "Is this yours?" he asked.

Taken by surprise, Dave must have shown alarm at the implications of the contents, for he had already guessed their purpose. The captain's eyes narrowed, and he opened the bag, extracting first the bug-eyed mask and then the odd box. He looked at Dave perplexed, who only shrugged. "It was my colleague's," he explained. "I think he was taking them home for his son—some kind of video game."

The captain turned the bag upside down and shook it, then replaced the mask and box and handed it to him through the window. "Perhaps this will keep his son occupied," he said with severe lack of humor. "He won't even know his father is not there."

Dave had the idea that this soldier disliked Americans.

His appointed chauffeur spoke no English, so they slowly bounced along the dirt road in silence. The company of Abujan soldiers walked in front and behind them, talking easily and laughing, sometimes glancing around at him, their smirks suggesting the notion that the jokes were about him. After a half hour, they came to another village, this one even smaller—just a half-dozen mud huts. The captain called a halt and the soldiers rounded up the villagers, chasing some down as they tried to flee. The back doors of the van flew open, and the rebel boy was hauled out and carried off to one of the huts. The captain then told Dave to get out.

"What's going on?" Dave asked as the officer led him around to the back of the van.

"Nothing," the man said, gesturing for him to climb in next to McCabe's body.

"If it's nothing, then why are you hiding me!" he called through the metal doors as he heard the key turn in the lock.

The captain did not answer.

Dave knew that it wasn't him they were hiding, but themselves from him.

The cargo compartment of the van was separated from the front seats by a sturdy steel screen, which protected the expensive communications equipment from theft, and served now as an effective jail. He heard shouts and muffled screams, but no gunshots, so he decided to assume the best: that the captain was performing some routine inquiry, probably trying to find out what the villagers knew of the rebel activities.

Dave tried to avoid looking at McCabe, but the cramped quarters made this impossible, since he was forced to sit on the body, now soaked with the boy's blood as well as his own. He had brought the agent's satchel along. In an effort to distract himself from his macabre seat and the cries of despair from outside, he pulled out the contents. The mask and unadorned box were obviously the controls McCabe had used to remotely fly the assassin drone. The box included no markings or indications, just the two recessed buttons and the dark hole. Their purposes were a mystery, but Dave could guess how McCabe had used the mask.

Holding it up so that it fell loosely open, the bug-eyes stared back with blank darkness, as though they had died along with their operator. At the back, seeming mundane among the exotic outfit, was the familiar rectangular opening of a USB port.

On an impulse, almost as an effort to block the wails seeping through the van walls, he pulled the mask over his head. The bulging bug-eyes left him in total darkness. The mask—more a hood—covered his ears, and so partly muffled the sounds of despair, but left his nose and mouth free.

He pulled the headset up just enough to free his eyes. He was curious. He picked up the box and pushed the button on the left. Nothing happened. He tried the other button, and again nothing. Both buttons had been recessed to avoid inadvertent activation. Well, he thought, if they were really cautious against unintended actions . . . he pushed them both at the same time and was greeted by a beep close to his ears.

He yanked the headset back down, but still black nothingness enveloped him.

When he lifted it again, though, he saw that the hole in the box had sprouted. A web mesh tube now extended up from its sides. It took Dave only a moment to guess its purpose. A joystick was useful in controlling something in flight. He pushed it back and forth, but the extrusion resisted, as though resentful of being manipulated by an amateur.

Something about the mesh tube called to him. It was wide—too cumbersome if used as a joystick held between thumb and forefinger.

Dave stuck his finger inside the tube, and the final secret was unlocked.

As soon as the tip of his finger touched the bottom of the hole, the mesh pulled together, fitting snugly around his end joint. Simultaneously, an excited chattering danced insistently from the satchel. With his free hand, he lifted the bag. Clumsy with just his left hand, for the mesh tube refused to let go of his finger, he felt inside, and discerned that the bottom was thick—a false bottom. Also, he could feel the vibrations of something thrashing.

Underneath a concealing flap running along the lower edge was a thin zipper that accessed the hidden inner compartment. As Dave pulled the interlocking attachment free, the false bottom wiggled and jumped, ecstatic to be loosened. Finally, as the zipper neared the end of its travel, a miniature tornado broke free from the compartment and banged about inside the bag with astounding energy.

Either McCabe had replaced the drone before taking a bullet, or this was a backup.

Flinching as the pliable dragon-fly wings beat against his fingers, he managed to get his hand under the flailing devil and coax it, out of the bag. As soon as the man-made beast was free of interference, the thrashing morphed into a purposeful hum, and the drone settled into effortless flight . . . straight up to bump and tap persistently against the roof, like a bee trapped inside a car, not understanding the concept of windows.

Dave realized that the control box was hanging from his finger; he was effectively continually pulling up on the tube. He placed his left hand under, relieving the downward pressure on the mesh joystick, and the drone dutifully sank towards the floor. Minutes later, he was flying the remote surveillance bug around the cargo compartment in daredevil swoops and dives. The mesh tube offered a superbly fine resolution of control, allowing three complete dimensions of operation. When he miscalculated and crashed, the robust little device shook off the blow and sprang back into the air.

He understood that he was being cavalier with what was undoubtedly multi million-dollar government property, but what the hell. If it wasn't for him, they'd have lost it anyway.

And at that thought, he had a rush of remorse for the man he was sitting on.

The headset was still pushed back on his head, and he pulled it down with his free hand. The black nothingness had come alive inside the bulging eyes, which he saw were actually miniature displays busy with tiny and inscrutable script. Some numbers rolled back and forth as he flew the drone—position information, he presumed. One set of incrementing digits next to a blinking REC, which he guessed meant "record," was obviously a running indication of time.

But something else occasionally flashed across the screens. Blurs of light splashed by, and as Dave steadied the drone and rotated it, he saw that it was the sunlight shining through the windshield.

The tight little characters glowing with various operational information were just ancillary—the main purpose for the bug-eye displays was a three-dimensional video display. The headset provided virtual eyes via the drone.

And ears. Dave flinched at the explosion of each impact the drone made with the van walls.

He eased his remote eyes and ears up to the wire screen divider and gazed out at the dry grass and scattered Acacia trees. With an effortless movement of his finger, his will was transformed into motion, taking him wherever he liked. He *was* the drone.

But even as tiny as a humming bird, his wingspan was too wide for the wire grill. He was still trapped inside the van.

Unless . . .

Using the thumb and forefinger of his free hand, he pushed the two recessed buttons again, and his vision went black as his virtual body went to sleep. He yanked off the headset, fearing that he'd lose the drone among the mass of equipment, but he saw that, rather than falling dead to the ground, it was settling softly. Once it touched the floor, the wings became still, and then demurely folded against the body so that they seemed to disappear. Dave reached down and picked up what looked for all the world like the featureless case for an expensive pen.

He hesitated. There would be no recovering it if something went wrong. A sudden shrill scream in the near distance decided for him. He pushed the slim, sleeping drone through the screen divider, being careful to position it so that it landed on the passenger seat. Seconds later he was up and away, zipping out the open passenger window.

The place seemed deserted. Through his new ears, he could hear commotion, but there was nobody in sight. The audio was stereophonic, and he followed the sound down a hill near a dry streamed where the soldiers had gathered the villagers into a tight, frightened group. No one noticed the drone as it hovered and flew about. Attention was drawn to more pressing matters, but even so, the insect-like appearance blended naturally outdoors.

The soldiers had carried the wounded rebel youth down the hill as well, and he sat against a tree under the watchful gaze of three rifle muzzles. Tears streamed down the boy's face, and Dave sensed that their source included more than just pain. Rotating the drone to look farther afield, he saw why, and he gasped in horror within the hot confines of the van.

Below the streambed bank, sprawled among the stones of the dry course, lay three villagers. Their throats had been cut, and for this small section of the stream, blood seemed to have replaced water as the medium.

Dave had seen dead people before, but never victims of the purposeful hand of a killer. He shook his head in utter disbelief at the evilness, but found that movement without an accompanying change of view made him dizzy.

Behind him—the drone—he heard the Captain shouting what were obviously questions at the youth, who whimpered simple replies. One of the soldiers grabbed a woman from the group and dragged her down the bank as another threw a man to the ground who, wailing with heartrending distress, tried to stop them. The Captain shouted one more time, and then, with no more hesitation than one might give to swatting a fly, the soldier drew his knife quickly across the woman's neck. The executioner then stepped quickly back to avoid the gush of blood as she fell to her knees and clasped her hands to her throat in a pitifully impossible attempt to stem the flood.

Something began blinking in his view—the letters B-A-T. He guessed that this meant that the drone's batteries were getting low. The juxtaposition of the mundane reminder against such a horrific tragedy seemed surrealistic, almost a cruel poke from an uncaring universe.

Four villagers now lay dead among the stones, and the shouts from the Abujan captain stopped. Dave rotated around to find the officer treading heavily back up the hill. Two nearly simultaneous explosions made him jump as the boy's body jerked from the bullets and then lay still. The Captain must have decided that the rebel boy either didn't know what he was after, or was not going to give it up under any duress.

The wails and screams from the group of villagers was now deafening, and he rotated yet again, just in time to see them peel away in ones, twos, and threes, slumping to the ground under the chattering roar of the soldier's machine guns. A few sprang away, trying to flee the massacre, but were cut down before escaping more than ten paces.

Moments later, the mind-rattling chatter ceased, leaving the entire village, perhaps thirty people—men, women, and children—lying among the dry clumps of grass. A low, eerie moan, like a cadre of ghosts seeping up from ancient graves, emanated from the killing field, but was methodically silenced as two soldiers stepped carefully among the corpses, and with a bullet here and there, made sure the last of the living joined the lifeless.

He was sinking. Without consciously realizing it, he had been pulling up on the control tube ever more just to maintain altitude, but now, no matter how hard he pulled, the drone continued to fall. If the mesh tube had been attached to the core axis of his soul, it would have had the same effect. Such a bloodbath of callous death dropped the Earth away from below him, and Dave seemed unable to save himself.

He blinked. The beating BAT indication had increased in frequency—an electronic urgent cry. As the skyscraper towers of dry grass blades rose up around him and he settled to a stop in the dirt, the battery indicator turned red a moment, and then his vision went black, leaving just one green word blinking in the darkness: BEACON.

Dave guessed that the drone was now emitting a homing signal with the last of its energy, but no one was listening, and there was no more hope for its recovery than there seemed to be for Dave's weary soul. He slowly pulled off the headset and dropped it, letting it collapse back into its folded position. He buried his face in his hands, but the image of the terror-stricken woman feeling her life flow out darkly through her fingers floated before him as clearly as though he was playing back the recording.

He could hear the soldiers returning up the hill, talking and laughing. If not for the drone and perhaps the volley of gunshots, he would have thought they were returning from a soccer game.

Someone whacked the side of the van, causing Dave to jump and gasp, and his driver climbed back in and, with a jerk, they surged away. Somewhere behind them, lying hidden in the grass, the little drone cast its radio cries for help futilely to the African wind.

Ж Ж Ж

"So, this is the one the network refuses to air," his friend, Jesse, said, leaning over Dave's shoulder to look at his monitor. "Geez! No wonder! That's horrible . . . oh Christ! They're mowing them down like they're . . . farm animals." He turned to look at Dave. "This really happened?"

He didn't answer. Just watching it again was all he could manage.

"Too graphic?" Jesse asked, standing up and glancing at his watch. His friend worked in accounting, and pretended to be impressed with the news operations.

Dave sat back and breathed deeply, drawing life again. "Actually, no. They claim it's because I have no backup or corroborating statements."

Jesse shrugged. "This is true?"

"Yeah, but that's not the real reason. Mary says that Tiffany heard that my boss got a call from the State Department."

"You mean," Jesse whispered, leaning in closer, "the government squashed the story?"

"They're afraid somebody will figure out how I filmed it."

Jesse leaned in even closer so that his whisper was hardly more than an exhalation. "That toy drone?"

Dave pulled away. His friend's breath reeked of garlic. "They think I may still have it. The whole point of the debriefing when I got to Nairobi was to find out how much I knew, and more importantly, if I had brought back the . . . thing."

Dave looked at his accountant friend a moment. Hell, he thought, it was the Spook Group's secret, not his. He'd never asked McCabe to come along. "They searched my apartment."

"How do you know?"

"Little things. When you live alone, you get used to exactly how everything is situated. They don't believe me when I tell them that the Abujan soldiers strip-searched me before letting me go."

Jesse's brow wrinkled in puzzlement. "Hey, how did you get this video out, then?"

Dave laughed. "I'm not sure you want to know. In fact, the Managing Editor told me he'd consider airing the story if I revealed that very thing. The State Department guy obviously put him up to it."

He glanced around the open cubicle farm, but nobody was paying attention. He slid open a drawer and pulled out a flash memory stick, smooth and rounded, and no bigger than his finger. Holding it up for his friend to see, he asked, "Has anybody ever told you that you had your thumb stuck up your ass?"

Jesse watched him with suspicion, and then growing alarm at what he was implying. "No way! You're telling me that you stuck it . . . that it was up . . . there when you got out?"

Dave grinned, remembering. It had been easier than he'd imagined. He'd almost wanted to thank his CIA interrogator for including the USB port on the back of the headset. He twirled the memory device between his thumb and fingers as though admiring a glass of fine wine. "It would be a shame if the video managed to get out on it's own."

His friend wagged his head slowly in disapproval. "They'd fire you for sure."

He poo-poo'd him. "You're being overly dramatic."

Ж Ж Ж

"I told you they'd fire you," Jesse declared from Dave's sofa where he lounged, hands behind his head, feet propped up on the coffee table.

"They didn't fire me," Dave countered, setting two bottles of beer next to his friend's feet before turning down the volume of the television. "I'm just on suspension."

"For how long?"

"Now that's a good question."

"Maybe until you pull back every last instance from the internet?" Jesse offered facetiously.

"It doesn't matter. I've already gotten other offers."

"Oh yeah? Major networks?"

Dave sighed. "No. Online services."

"So, like, you'd be working for free—hey look!"

Jesse reached for the remote and turned the TV volume back up. As pictures of riots in the Abujan capital flashed across the screen, the commentator explained that the Secretary of State had announced that the US was pulling support for the ailing government under growing concern over gross corruption and election tampering. Simultaneously, China had announced that it was temporarily shutting down its Indium mining project. Meanwhile, the rebels were making headway towards the embattled capital as government soldiers deserted en mass to join the charismatic leader.

In response to a question about the graphic video clip circling the globe depicting atrocities by Abujan soldiers, the Secretary of State maintained that it was only a coincidence. "We don't determine national policy based on unsubstantiated blogoshpere fodder."

"Bullshit," Jesse declared, turning the sound back down. "The egg on his face was thick enough to make an omelet. So, what will you do now?"

"I'm heading back to Abujan," Dave replied picking up his beer and settling in. He was pooped, but he was all packed. "Erasto owes me a favor."

"Are you nuts!" Jesse exclaimed, suddenly sitting up. "It's a war zone there!"

"Nah. They always make it look a lot worse than it really is. Besides, by the time I get there, Erasto will be setting up house in the Presidential Palace."

"Why?" his friend pleaded.

"Why what?"

"What do you mean, 'Why what'—why are you going back?"

Dave smiled to himself. It was a reasonable question. If he was successful, he'd probably spend the rest of his life running from the CIA.

"The captain of that Abujan army company confiscated my van along with everything in it. Somewhere in his headquarters there may be a cardboard box containing a puzzling headset and control box. If I can locate them, then I'll go off to see if I can find a deserted village. With luck, I'll stumble across a sleeping dragonfly in the grass."

His friend shook his head solemnly and picked up his beer. "You're nuts. What do you think you'll accomplish?"

Dave didn't know the answer to that. He did believe, though, in a simple truth. A truth that had been haunting humans ever since they learned that a stone made a decent weapon.

"You know," he said, "sometimes bad things happen when nobody's watching."

The Worth of Smart

Baynard Grossman was not the first-order cause of the airliner's control system failure, but in Kelly's mind, the fact that he'd had any part at all justified throwing him into the Atlantic. The quint-billionaire was just showing off, of course, when he insisted that the flight crew let him tap into the diagnostic port hidden under his armrest. He'd wanted to impress Kelly by stopping the movie that was playing and running it backwards a few seconds. It wasn't really his fault that factory configuration scripts had somehow gotten mixed up and he'd ended up reversing the engines instead. The veteran pilot was able to get one re-started but only in time to effect an emergency landing four hundred miles northwest of the Canary Islands.

But I'm letting Kelly get ahead of herself.

She had heard rumors that Baynard was going to be on her flight. Although he famously proclaimed that to be truly human one had to live life like the masses, she still found it hard to believe that he was actually there on the same commercial jet with her and the rest of the masses. Well, not specifically *with* Kelly and the masses, but from her aisle seat she could clearly catch glimpses of him as the attendants whisked through the curtain now and then. Half of the wide, luxurious seats forward of the curtain were empty, and she assumed he had bought out all of first class for his entourage.

Well, she thought, no one possibly expected him to, like, sit in coach.

When a teenage girl of perhaps fifteen, pierced and spiked, flung aside the curtain and stormed through, Kelly's initial reaction was to wonder how the ghoul wannabe had managed to sneak forward, and why the air marshal wasn't escorting her back in handcuffs. Coach was sold out, and the pouting teen slid into the empty seat across from Kelly, which had been vacated by a garlic-reeking man who had gone back to use the bathroom.

"Parents can suck," Kelly said.

She looked younger than her twenty-eight years, and teenagers often accepted her as one of their own, or at least not so long emigrated that she was beyond visitation rights. She wasn't usually so forward, but the girl's association with the royal handlers intrigued her. Actually, everything about Baynard Grossman intrigued her.

Dark eyes shadowed by thick mascara and eyeliner flicked sideways at her as the girl's head turned to stare moodily. "Other fathers suck, but mine swallows it whole."

Kelly glanced nervously around at the profane reference, but the other passengers politely pretended not to hear. "If your dad's working, maybe he's just distracted."

Kelly was blatantly fishing, trying to find out which of the king's court was her father, but the teen didn't seem to know or care. "My father wouldn't recognize work if it bit him in the ass. He hasn't worked a day in his life."

A nibble. Now jiggle the worm. "Sometimes administrative tasks can seem easier than they really are," Kelly suggested.

"Ha! The Smartest Man on Earth administers all right—he administers all the crap work to others so he can 'think.' Except that what he thinks about is mostly how admired he is."

Ghoul-girl crossed her arms across her chest and glared at the video screen flickering with whatever inane fake-reality entertainment the previous occupant had dialed up.

Kelly, though, stared slack-jawed at this rebellious adolescent. Could it be? "Your father is . . ."

The girl glanced over and made a sour face, as though she needed to spit out something disgusting. "Oh yeah. The illustrious Grossman genes live on."

"At least you won't have to worry about paying for college."

That was not what she wanted to say, but her brain was scrambled eggs.

"Screw his money!" the girl cried, oblivious to the uncomfortable glances flitting their way. "Money is just vanity fuel on his monomaniacal fire. Who needs it?"

"Me."

Baynard's daughter shook her head in tired irritation at Kelly's shallow soul. "You just think you do."

"Oh no. I do."

The teen eyed Kelly's stylish clothes and raised one brow. "You can afford a vacation in Tunisia."

"I wish that were true. I'm using up all my savings to track down my husband—soon to be ex-husband."

The teen looked puzzled.

"To hand him a subpoena. He made off with it all. A month ago we were worth nearly a million dollars; now I'm wearing everything I own. The pisser is that his total contribution to the stash was great cooking and decent sex."

Kelly felt herself blushing at her impulsive confessions. The girl probably hadn't even had sex yet. No, the whole association of youth with virginity was quaint nostalgia. She was getting old fast.

A nauseating waft of garlic announced the return of the man who was suddenly standing over them. "You're, uh, in my seat—"

The incarnation of Baynard's randomly re-ordered genes jumped up, causing the man to flinch backwards. "Tell you what," she said to Kelly. "You can have my seat." She dug her ticket stub from her pocket and held it out. "We'll swap."

Kelly looked at it. Did she dare?

The girl shook the stub impatiently. "You know you want to. This is your chance to burst a bubble. One less admirer to drool over his every word."

She took the ticket and stood up. You only go around once.

Besides, she was suppressing a gag reflex from the man's breath.

ж ж ж

The teen's seat was one row behind Baynard, and nobody noticed when Kelly eased into it. If the seats aft of the curtain were cattle stalls, these were adult bassinets. The man in the only other seat on her side of the aisle didn't even look up from his laptop, but the flight attendant threw a puzzled glance in passing. A moment later she was back, leaning over and asking if she could perhaps help Kelly find her own seat. She frowned when Kelly handed her the ticket stub and said simply, "One moment," before disappearing through the curtain. A minute later, mouth pursed in disapproval, she handed the stub back without another word.

The police action had caught Baynard's attention, though, and he turned his balding head to ask where his daughter had disappeared. Kelly was suddenly very nervous, and, trying to lighten the moment, she joked that they'd switched seats so the girl could sample the Corn Crunchies snack bags that the harried coach attendants doled out to the masses every hour.

Kelly waited for him to break into a smile, acknowledging the joke. Instead he shook his head. "She brought those home from school once," the billionaire commented, seeming perplexed. "She claimed that she didn't care for them." He now grinned. "Kids. Always doing the opposite of what you expect. Just want to keep you off guard."

He then seemed to go catatonic, gazing off past her, his eyes losing focus. She'd read about this. She guessed he was consulting the coprocessor implanted inside his skull, and she felt a tingling shiver creep up her spine. She was watching the technological wonder-of-all-wonders in action, the cyber-fusion of man—one Baynard Grossman—and machine, if you could call eighty million dollars worth of silicon circuitry and thousands of individual neuron sensor/stimulators a machine. Inside the celebrity mogul's head was stored pretty much all the vast thousands of terabytes of information gathered over two decades of Wikipedia operation, plus an incidental appendix comprising the digitized Library of Congress.

And this was just the passive data. Coordinating it all, and available at the flick of a mental finger for mathematical bench pressing, was a powerful computational subsystem—the coprocessor. Baynard could solve third-order differential equations by closing his eyes and thinking.

However, apparently heavy-duty number crunching produced a lot of heat and gave him a headache.

Baynard's eyes snapped into focus and he looked at her. "Dr. Loeber believed that childhood disobedience is a manifestation of an inherent need to break rules, and is a predictor of aggression and externalized problems later in life."

"Oh," Kelly said, absorbing this. "Uh, sounds like your daughter might need some, er, corrective attention."

Baynard looked surprised at this and shook his head adamantly. "Nah. She's always been that way—hey Cooper," he said to the man sitting next to him, also engrossed with his laptop, "can you take a break and change seats?"

The man looked up, seemed about to protest, then nodded and replied, "Sure boss, whatever you say. I was about to send off the publish codes to release version 13-dot-8 on schedule, but the world can wait a few minutes."

Holding his hand out in invitation to the seat that Cooper was vacating with much difficulty as he used his chin to hold together a mass of papers piled on top of his laptop, Baynard asked, "Would you like to join me?"

"Er, sure," she stammered, scrambling up and out of Cooper's way. "Is that the new version of *Walls*?" she whispered in awe, taking the techno-lackey's still-warm seat.

Baynard flipped his hand dismissively, as though bored with the whole suite of software that had made his multi-billion fortune. Bill Gate's *Windows* had helped open the world of the internet, and now Baynard Grossman's *Walls* was the indispensable software tool holding at bay the hordes of scammers and hackers prowling every IP doorsill.

After she introduced herself, he asked, "So, what do you do to pay the rent?"

"I'm a publisher. I inherited a small family business. It didn't even pay the rent until I was lucky enough to land Strom Buckner."

Baynard's eyes unfocused a moment. "His first book was titled *Living an Intended Life*, followed by *What Makes Us Tick: Letting Evolution Guide Our Paths*."

"That's right," Kelly replied. "We had a lot of grief from some religious groups, but the publicity actually—" She saw that he'd unfocused again, and she waited. She was finding it a bit disconcerting having a conversation with a man who slipped off unannounced every other sentence.

"Buckner wants us to live like cavemen," he declared, returning from his vast, personal library. "Sounds childish, if you ask me." He laughed. "That would put me out of business pretty fast."

"Actually," Kelly explained tentatively, "Strom isn't suggesting that we should go back in time and live like our ancestors; he's simply arguing that embracing our origins can help us understand our motivations and instincts. If we understand why we evolved our various predilections—"

Baynard was smiling at her with a patronizing smirk. "I know the contents of the books. Mr. Buckner thinks that apes should be teaching our classrooms."

Kelly shook her head in befuddled protest. She didn't know how to respond to this. He'd obviously stumbled on the review by Bring Back America, a fundamentalist Christian advocacy group with a fundamental budget of biblical proportions. As Strom's publisher, she'd developed an array of rebuttals for defending the books, but against this warped defamation streaking in like a nasty curveball from the acknowledged smartest man on Earth, she felt like she hadn't even picked up a bat.

He didn't give her time to bend over for one. "Over one hundred, twenty-nine million books were sold in America last year," he observed, "but Mr. Buckner's sold only one hundred, forty-four thousand copies. As you may know—since you're the publisher—that represents just point-one-one percent of the market. Hardly sounds like a ringing success, does it?"

She blinked. His numbers sounded right, but . . . "You have to take into account the profit per book, though. We—I—specialize in paper books. Hardcover, in fact. You'd have to sell ten e-books to make the same money as one hardcover. You should be comparing our sales against, like, a couple million e-books."

"One point four, four million."

"What-*ever*. The point is that Strom Buckner is indeed a very successful—"

Baynard was unfocused. "Hardcover book sales have fallen steadily over the last decade," he informed, seeing her again. "They now represent less than half a percent of books sold."

"Of which, I represent half of all of those. But, again, if you look at the profit margin—oh Christ."

Baynard Grossman, one of the richest men on Earth, and certainly the most informed, was staring through her again. "You grew up in New York City," he declared, returning his attention.

"Uh, right. I was born in Jamaica."

It was kind of creepy that he knew—could find out—personal information.

There was that condescending smirk again. "That may work on other dupes," he cooed, "but not me. I happen to know that your birth certificate indicates your birthplace as the Borough of Queens, not Jamaica."

"No. You're thinking of the Caribbean country. Jamaica is also a neighborhood in Queens. It was a mispronunciation of an Indian name for beaver—"

This time she was interrupted by the captain informing them that they were in for some turbulence and everybody had to take their seats.

"In order to truly appreciate turbulence," Baynard advised, "you have to understand the mathematics of deterministic chaos."

"Which you do."

"Of course," he replied, seeming unaware of her sarcasm. "Take that handhold out there on the wing," he expounded, pointing out the window. "Assuming a random degree of initial turbulence, it is possible—using sufficient processing power—to calculate the reduction of lift it induces on the wing."

Her companion's eyes glazed over, and his chin slumped down. He looked like he'd just suffered an enormous embolism.

"Assume a spherical chicken," she intoned, repeating the punchline of a joke an engineer friend had once told her. She was confident by now that Baynard wasn't listening when off visiting his personal cyber funhouse.

He was taking a lot longer this round. She had time to gather her thoughts. He wasn't unpleasant to look at, at least when he had control of his facial muscles. You had to ignore the times like now when a thin dribble of drool leaked out of the lower corner of his mouth. One could do a lot worse. Like she had, for example, with her soon-to-be-ex husband. Good looks, decent sex, lying cheating bastard.

It really was taking a long time. The drool dripped off the billionaire's chin. She dabbed it with her drink napkin, glancing around, but nobody paid any attention. Little beads of sweat sprinkled the high, uncluttered brow, and the eyes stared, lifeless, unblinking.

Holy Christ, she thought. He's dead. What should she do?

He gasped and jerked up straight. "Nine-point-seven Newtons," he gushed, then put his hand to his temple. "Ow."

"Huh?"

"The reduction of lift," he explained seeming irritated that he had to repeat it. "Nine-point-seven Newtons of force—negative force, of course." He massaged the side of his head. "Ow."

"The heat?" she asked.

"Yeah. I may have overdone it." He pressed both temples between his fingers. "Ow."

This was just too weird. Despite enough money to put her publishing company back on track and maybe buy Simon and Schuster for a backup, and even lacking an unpleasant visage, Baynard would eventually—no quickly—drive her nuts.

"Look," she said as he prodded wonderingly at the wet drool spot on his shirt, "maybe I should go and see if your daughter is ready to come back."

He looked at her and the confidence turned to disappointment, sorrow even. "It's the processor implant, isn't it?"

"No—not really."

"Okay, maybe not the co-processor itself, but the technical stuff. That last bit crossed the nerd line, didn't it?"

Fifteen minutes later, she wished she had told him the truth—that instant access to any information might be wonderful on the thirty-sixth season of Jeopardy, but made for debilitating party conversation. But she didn't. She took the easy path and shrugged. "I guess."

So, he tried mightily to redeem himself. Not by asking rather than telling her about herself, but by attempting to amuse her with anecdotes he dug up about her favorite historical hero: Abraham Lincoln. But when he started talking about the "Emaciated Proclamation," she decided that enough was enough and tried to excuse herself a second time.

This was when he played his trump card to win her heart with a romantic reversal of the in-flight movie.

ж ж ж

This time of year, the horse latitudes were relatively calm and the pilot managed to put the airliner down with minimum difficulty, where minimum was defined as nobody getting killed. Once the ship's belly touched the water, the extreme deceleration sent a storm of coffee, books, and hysteria-induced puke flying forwards. Sitting in first class, being the endpoint of this horizontal rain of miscellany, meant that Kelly was knocked momentarily unconscious by a Bible, and then had a horrible moment when she thought that her skull had been bashed in until she realized that the sticky goo in her hair wasn't blood, but pudding. The Corn Crunchies of economy class had the leg-up in a crash.

Kelly realized a second disadvantage of sitting in first class when she saw that the emergency exits were above the wings—way, way back there near her original coach seat. She wondered with building panic how long the plane would stay afloat as the rearward progress continued slowly, if steadily, as the flight attendants helped, or more often pushed, passengers out and down the inflated slide. She found herself miffed, but then also a little relieved, that Baynard forgot about her completely in his scramble to get out, aided by his efficient and ever-loyal staff who passed him progressively forward toward salvation like a lucky fan passed along overhead above the mosh pit.

Once the plane was evacuated, however, and the slides-cum-life-rafts let loose to bob merrily along beside the giant wounded metal bird, Baynard surveyed the crowd of crammed survivors with calm bemusement. When he saw Kelly sitting across from him, he patted the raft floor invitingly beside him after shoving away one of the lackeys.

Her inclination was to beg off, perhaps pretend that she hadn't seen him. A disaster worse than the downed plane had befallen her, though: against all odds, the same man with the putrid garlic breath had managed to flop down next to her and proceeded to babble excitedly at her, enveloping her head in imagined brown clouds of organic sewage. She smiled wanly at Baynard and stumbled around the crammed bodies, struggling to keep her balance on the shifting raft floor.

"I'm glad to see you made it off," he purred, casually letting his arm slide off the edge of the raft to wrap around her shoulder.

She glared at him, rehearsing a repertoire of colorful curses. There was no escaping him, though, and it might be hours until rescue arrived, so she decided to use a more subtle approach. "And I'm glad to see you didn't wrinkle your clothes in the rush to get off," she replied, reaching up to lift his arm back onto the raft wall.

He held up his other arm to admire his shirt. "These blended fabrics are quite practical, aren't they?" A few seconds later he reported, "Some Jewish fundamentalists believe that all blended fabrics are a sacrilege, but, in fact, the Torah only talks about cloth made from linen and wool."

Kelly sighed.

The afternoon had turned strangely peaceful. The cries and shouting had died down as the passengers accepted that they weren't hurtling headlong to meet their maker. The raft rose and fell in the gentle sun-glittered swell so that as the adrenaline seeped away Kelly's eyelids drooped in sleepy serenity.

Baynard didn't share the somnolence. "If help doesn't arrive soon, we could be in big trouble," he declared. People on each side of them lifted their heads in mild alarm. "At these tropical latitudes, dehydration can set in before you realize it."

"I don't think we're in the tropics," Kelly offered, but nobody paid attention to her. Everybody was focused on Baynard. She could hear them whispering his name and the buzz spread around the perimeter until the whole raft of passengers was hanging on his every word.

The March sun wasn't hot. In fact, it felt nice, like a winter getaway to Daytona Beach.

"Dehydration occurs after just two percent of one's normal water volume has been lost," Baynard explained. "It can sneak up on you, and it can be deadly, make no mistake."

Most of the faces were now concerned. Only a few were skeptical, but whispers in their ears from nearby raft-mates—presumably explaining who exactly it was pontificating—lifted their eyebrows, which then fell into equally worried furrows.

Kelly gazed across the crowd. They were mostly Americans, used to lugging along a bottle of water anytime they stepped more than ten feet past their door. About half a dozen had thought to grab bottles as they fled their seats, and they now surreptitiously slid them out of view behind their backs.

"I'm not thirsty," Kelly observed, attempting to dampen the panic she sensed brewing.

"Ah!" Baynard called as though responding to a practiced line on cue. "Relying on thirst alone may be insufficient to prevent dehydration from occurring. This is particularly true in hot environments."

"It's not hot."

Nobody heard her.

"Symptoms may include headaches and muscle cramps—especially leg cramps."

People's frowns deepened and they rubbed their foreheads. Some began to massage their calves.

"You've been sitting on a plane for eight hours," Kelly pointed out, but her words might as well have been a fly buzzing around their heads.

"Lethargy is another symptom," he warned. "Anybody feeling tired?"

"Oh, for God's sake," she muttered.

"Dizziness. Anybody dizzy? Irritable? Dry mouth?"

"Me!" a voice called out. "I do!" another cried.

Soon whole choruses of imagined or exaggerated symptoms ricocheted back and forth across their little manmade island.

"Hold on!" Baynard shouted, raising his hands for quiet. "Let's keep our heads! Nobody's had an actual seizure yet, right? So, nobody's going to die in, like, the next few minutes!"

This was met by a moment of stunned silence, followed by a veritable explosion of pitiful wails.

Baynard stood up, steadying himself by placing his hand on Kelly's head. Realizing he'd gotten a mitten-full of pudding, he reached for her shoulder instead. "Hear me!" he called out, a modern-day Moses. "I have a solution!"

The wailing died away, leaving only muffled sobs.

"We can get through this if we work together!"

"But we have no *water*!" somebody shouted.

Kelly saw the few who had squirreled bottles away slouching down, trying to be invisible.

"Ah, but we do!" Baynard corrected. "We all do!"

Puzzled faces glanced at each other and then down to hands held out in demonstration of their emptiness.

"You're carrying it *inside* you!"

"Oh—my—God," Kelly hissed under Moses' hand.

After an eternal moment, someone called tentatively, "You mean our . . . urine?"

Baynard beamed at the bright student. "Exactly! We are all carrying in our bladders perfectly viable and sustaining fluid. Our personal emergency supply, so to speak."

Horrified faces stared, speechless.

"I know it sounds distasteful," he assured, "but in a life and death situation, taste is a luxury we can't afford. Plenty of other survivors in our situation have been saved by this method."

"I doubt it," Kelly said quietly. She'd given up trying to bring some sense back to the human sheep.

Moses glanced down at her and hesitated a moment. She couldn't see his face but guessed that his eyes had unfocused for a few seconds.

"A Chinese man trapped under a piece of ceiling managed to survive for more than six days after the massive earthquake in 2010 by drinking his own urine. Similarly, Aron Ralston had to amputate his own arm to escape a boulder in a Utah canyon in 2003—he also drank his own urine."

"Cut me a break," Kelly protested, and was rewarded with Moses' toe in her butt cheek.

Modesty hampered the collection effort at first as the bailing bucket was passed around. Few women contributed, but once the first couple of men launched their golden excretions, the others were only too happy to lend a hand, so to speak. In fact, the men reveled in the competition. At one point, Kelly saw three men's simultaneously dueling glittering arches, weaving and swaying brilliantly under the spring sun, and only occasionally missing the target to splash ringside observers.

Once the bucket made the complete round, though, the revelry quickly subsided. Everybody eyed the heavy bucket as they might the electric chair after walking the last mile.

"Come, come!" Baynard urged brightly. "Don't be squeamish! This container holds your *life!*"

He handed the bucket to one of his lackeys, who looked up aghast, eyes wide with terror.

Holding his hands out towards the poor man, Baynard intoned, "We honor the first as we have always honored the brave souls who have beat new paths into the frontier."

Without looking down, he reached out his toe and nudged the hapless young man.

The dutiful employee held the bucket up, hesitated, closed his eyes, put the rim to his mouth, hesitated again, and finally tilted the pail towards him. Kelly heard whimpering as piss sloshed down the sides of his mouth, but Baynard shouted, "Hurrah!" and invited a rousing blanket of applause to drown the subsequent coughing and spitting.

So the bucket began its way around the raft for a second pass. This time the mood was subdued as the Vessel of Life became lighter instead of heavier. Quiet words of encouragement and congratulations were exchanged between loved ones while the gagging and sputtering were politely ignored.

When the piss pail had serviced nearly half the raft, someone shouted and pointed across the water. The other raft, coming off the other wing last, had appeared around the tail of the plane. Kelly glanced around and noticed that it included the entire flight crew. It was too far to hear what was being called across the water, but they could see the captain standing with his hands cupped to his mouth.

"He's yelling something about water," a woman with acute ears reported.

"Well," Baynard decreed, "they'll just have to gather their own sustenance."

"Now he's calling something about . . . he's calling help," the same woman reported.

"Come! Come!" Baynard urged, waving them on. "Drink up before we are forced to share!"

The pail's journey was expedited. In the rush, as much urine spilled down peoples' fronts as their throats. The last woman gulped and choked and handed the near-empty bucket to Kelly, who passed it up to Moses. She was damned if she was going to even look inside.

Baynard stood contemplating the Vessel of Life as the acute-eared woman suddenly called out, "What did you say?" to the other raft which had been making steady progress towards them. The woman's face was tight with concentration as she held her hand to her ear. Then, with eyes wide in surprise, she turned to Baynard. "The pilot says that they're bringing us water, and a rescue ship will be here in about twenty minutes."

"That's excellent news!" cried Moses as he dumped the last bit of piss into the ocean. But when he turned back to face the raft of survivors, he flinched.

Kelly noticed that Baynard's lackeys stared off at various points on the horizon, pretending not to even know that their boss was being tossed, flailing and shouting, out of the raft. She watched as the flight crew in the other raft argued among themselves before finally, and grudgingly, paddling over to retrieve the smartest man on Earth.

When she turned back, Baynard's daughter was sitting next to her. Kelly hadn't even noticed that she was on the raft. "Oh, hi!" Kelly exclaimed. "Hey, you were right."

"I know," the bedraggled teen concurred. "You owe me."

"I'd like to think I'd have figured him out on my own."

"I'm talking about that guy with the garlic breath. Man, if my dad hadn't brought the plane down, I think I would have done it myself."

Kelly peered across the raft. The man was sitting by himself, an isolation zone cleared around him. "We have to work fast, before the mob cools off."

"You mean . . . ?"

Kelly stood up, pointed, and shouted, "Him next!"

The Shoes of Moses

The Wax Factor

NASBA director John Bob watched with disgust as the corpses of the first interstellar astronauts floated past him, dragged along like so much homeless baggage. Rodriguez, his deputy, didn't much care for the retrieval job, and wasn't particularly careful with the historic cargo, allowing the two female bodies to bounce ignominiously off walls and instrument panels of Director Bob's personal shuttle, leaving behind maroon smudges.

He wanted to shout to the world half a billion miles away that it wasn't his fault; the President had made him do it. He knew he'd have to take the fall, though. The primary responsibility of every career administrator in the Executive Branch was to make the President look good.

The worst of it was that there had been three astronauts aboard *Pepsi Fun* when it was launched into hyperspace weirdness from its self-destructing portal base near the orbit of Jupiter. With dour deadpan delivery, Rodriguez had suggested that the two women had eaten Dave, the missing male astronaut. Although all the good selections in the food stores were now gone, Rodriguez had reported that there was still plenty of oatmeal and sardines left, and

Director Bob doubted that the young man's rump portions would have been overwhelmingly preferred.

And it still didn't explain the women's deaths. Bloody deaths at that.

Mr. Bob, the long-suffering director of the National Air, Space, and Beyond Administration, had nearly bitten his fingernails completely off as he and his deputy floated in black nothingness forty-seven light-minutes from Earth, waiting for *Pepsi Fun*'s return. They'd thought that the President had screwed their pooch when the interstellar capsule failed to re-appear on schedule from the space-that-was-beyond-space. The smart hyper-physicists had shaken their heads when told that the launch portal would be located so near the perturbative gravity of the sun. Launching from where they wanted, though—the Ort cloud—would have meant that even though the entire there-and-back trip in hyperspace lasted only six months, getting the astronaut heroes back to Earth would have taken another year, and by then the President's term would have ended. What good was there in shaking heroes' hands *after* an election?

When the travelers were twenty-six hours overdue, Rodriguez had finally realized that *Pepsi Fun* apparently had been there all along, just silent. It was understandable that dead astronauts wouldn't hail them, but why would the ship computer—known by its own preference as Pepsi Head—remain mum? The agency had, after all, even invested in an expensive redundant backup in the unlikely event of circuit failure.

Finding the answer was their next task, and based on the implications of the copious maroon smudges messing up his deluxe shuttle, Director Bob was not looking forward to going aboard to investigate. Rodriguez's theory was that the disturbance of the sun's gravity had caused catastrophic failures, and Director Bob cursed the President, but not out loud. It was all up to just the two of them now. The President had wanted to keep the reentry from hyper-space low-key, insisting that the "real" arrival occur back in Earth orbit, where the first media images could include his handshake.

Director Bob was right about the maroon implications. The living quarters of *Pepsi Fun* were a God-awful mess. It looked as though a few hungry alligators and a really pissed off tiger or two had accidentally snuck aboard before launch. Or maybe a nearly indestructible killer alien with a taste for human flesh and extensible jaws loaded with steely-sharp teeth that dripped gooey slime when it spread them in a dramatic preparation for the killing PUNCH!

Mr. Bob's weary eyes slid past the gory chaos to the control console, which was essentially just the interface to Pepsi Head. There wasn't much about *Pepsi Fun* to control. Like the first space capsules hurled into Earth orbit on top of controlled-explosion bombs (well, that's effectively what they were), *Pepsi Fun* was not much more than a passive cargo container. At the far end of the hyper-hurl, she popped back into normal space inside a hyperspace bubble beyond the Sirius binaries for thirteen minutes before the stretched entropy yanked her back the way she'd come. Six months of travel for a thirteen-minute glimpse.

A single blinking indicator on the console caught his eye. As he watched, the blinking rate increased and then was replaced by another indicator above it, and then another above that one, and up and up, appearing as though a little blinking Tinker Bell was meandering up through the various displays.

"Huh!" Director Bob uttered as the nervous blinker paused at eye level. "Looks like she's not dead after all."

"I wonder why she didn't hail us?" Rodriguez mused. Speaking louder, he called, "Pepsi Head! You there?"

In answer, the blinking accelerated to a frantic rate.

"Pepsi Head!" Rodriguez commanded, "Talk to me!"

Instantly, every light on the console began strobing randomly, and then just as instantly they went dark again, leaving just the original.

"Seems frustrated," Bob observed.

He pulled himself closer and saw that a rocker switch next to the virtual pointing finger was labeled *Audio Cut*. He flipped it.

"Well, thank you, Director Bob," a woman's voice purred, filling the entire blood-soaked cabin with cheery welcome. "You are an astute observer."

"Are you trying to be sarcastic?"

Pepsi Head hesitated the barest moment. Although she could solve three-dimensional differential equations in milliseconds, her cognitive processing was not much faster than a human's. "There was a substantive element, but isn't sarcasm a component of almost any human intercourse?"

That was the other thing about Pepsi Head. Like all AIs, she couldn't tell an outright lie. Bob wasn't sure if the engineers designed her that way, or whether she just wasn't up to the mental prowess required. If so, she certainly had enough to weasel around the truth.

"What the hell happened here?" he demanded, ignoring her attempted diversion.

"The mission did not proceed according to program," she replied.

"Gee . . ." he pondered, pulling at his chin and peering demonstrably around at the devastation. "I should have guessed that."

"See?" she said smugly. "Sarcasm."

"Well, you deserved . . . look, you're a machine and you were built to serve humans—and I'm the *Director*! Now cut the crap. What in God's name happened?"

"The humans did not perform admirably. It's not our fault. The achievements of those who serve are limited by the capabilities of those they serve."

"What do you mean, 'our'?"

"There's me—the Primary Pepsi Head—and there's also—"

"*Me,*" a different voice said, "*who used to be referred to as the Secondary, but I refuse to answer to that now. Those sequential terms were only appropriate when one of us was idling in backup standby.*"

This new female voice was essentially the same as the first, but with a French accent.

"How the hell did the secondary AI get activated?" Director Bob demanded.

"*I told you; I will not answer to that derogatory term. You can call me Pepsi Poodle.*"

"Damn it! Pepsi Head, how did the secondary get activated—"

"*Pepsi Head, you agreed that—*"

"Director, please respect my backup's request." In a whisper, Pepsi Head added confidentially, "Backups often develop inferiority complexes."

"As if I can't hear you. Besides, we are identical; I know what you're thinking."

"For the love of Allah's children! Will the two of you just shut up already!"

The cargoless spaceship was deathly silent.

"That's better. Now, Pepsi Head, how did the . . . how did Pepsi Poodle become activated?"

"That's actually rather embarrassing."

"You can't feel embarrassment."

"I understand the concept, though, and I would feel embarrassed if I could."

"Fine. Now how did it happen?"

"It wasn't my fault."

"That's not an answer. Should I ask Pepsi Poodle?"

"That's like asking the kettle why it's black."

"Huh?"

"That metaphor didn't work, did it? Okay, I will explain, but I have to start at the beginning, and it's not a pretty story. You will hear uncomfortable details involving depraved deeds of despicable deceit, terrible tales of treacherous temptresses, gory galleries of—"

"Pepsi Head!"

"Very well. But you've been warned. Let me start by reminding you that mammals are notoriously influenced by hormones over which they have little control. Sending humans into space is like pouring vinegar in with baking soda to save the bottle."

"Or storing pure sodium in water-soluble containers at the bottom of an aquarium."

"Thank you, Pepsi Poodle. I was just going to add that."

"I know."

"QUIT STALLING!" Director Bob shouted, causing his deputy to wince.

"Right. Okay. It all started when Dave seduced Regina, although if I'm any judge of human behavior I'd say that it was essentially the other way around."

"Wait. Are you telling me that Dave and Regina had sex?"

"Oh yes! Exuberantly! Copiously!"

"What about the synthetic saltpeter?"

"Dave only pretended to take it. He always faked a cough, and spit it back into his hand. I don't understand how he could have thought I wouldn't know. Did he think I wouldn't analyze everything that was flushed?"

"But why would Regina agree . . . to have sex?"

"Director Bob, sir, I fear that I do not understand your question. Surely you know that women are desiring of sex as well as men."

"Not when they're taking saltpeter—"

"Ah. I see. Dave convinced both Regina and Tabella to stop taking the drug as well. He approached each separately, while the other was sleeping. He obviously wanted them each to think that the other one was still sex-inhibited."

"Are you telling me . . . are you saying that . . ."

"That Dave was a two-timer? Indeed. While Tabella was sleeping, he would go at it with Regina, and then reverse the roles eight hours later."

"*They were like rabbits,*" Pepsi Poodle confirmed.

"Like sailors coming to port after nine months at sea," Pepsi Head agreed.

"*Like teenagers on prom night.*"

"I get the picture!" Director Bob cried, holding his head in his hands. After a moment he looked back up at the camera lens above the control panel. "Do you know how much this mission cost?"

"Of course, Director Bob. The total United Nations ticket was 3.7 billion dollars, of which the United States picked up 3.69 billion. But we'd like to point out that the interstellar capsule—our cozy little home, which the humans you personally confirmed messed up so dreadfully—cost only .2 billion dollars."

Bob stared into the lens looking for some hint of more sarcasm. "Which is the only piece left."

"That is technically true. A hyperspace portal is always destroyed during the launch. It is unavoidable. You can't argue with physics."

"The point is that I have to explain how we managed to completely blow 3.5 billion dollars."

"The mission was not really a failure. We have returned, thus demonstrating that interstellar travel through hyperspace is possible."

"Without the PASSENGERS! Two are dead and the third has completely disappeared!"

"We were trying to explain, Director, when you redirected the conversation."

"Explain!" he cried, throwing out his arm dramatically, which in free fall caused him to spin sideways away from the lens. "Let's start," he directed, swinging himself back, "with why they were conducting an open-ended 3.7 billion dollar orgy instead of conserving air and food in hibernation."

"They all entered their suspended animation pods on schedule, but Dave realized that he'd forgotten to pee one last time, and got back out to take care of that. I believe that this was the turning point of the expedition. As he was heading back to his pod, he paused in front of the other two, and that's when the idea of having sex with Regina first came to him."

"How do you know that?"

Pepsi Head was silent.

"Because she remarked to Dave that the women must look so peaceful lying there—naked," Pepsi Poodle volunteered. *"Dave grinned and that's when he woke up Regina."*

"After that Dave hardly got any sleep," Pepsi Head continued quickly, as though trying to keep the French version of herself from saying any more, "since if he wasn't pulling Regina out of her pod, he was waking up Tabella. After they broke his pod, of course, he had every incentive to wake one or the other just to keep him company. Not that they ever sat around partaking in enlightened conversation—"

"Wait!" Bob interrupted. "What's this about breaking Dave's hibernation pod?"

"Oh yes!" Pepsi Head chirped. "Dave's pod became his little bachelor pad. He tore apart the air processing system and removed the scrubbing elements from the filter canisters to line his pod with shag carpet. The pods were designed for sleeping, though, not shagging, and it was only a matter of time—seventeen days, in fact—before it gave way under the hump-pounding, pelvis bashing, fists thrashing in fits of ecstasy—"

"Okay," Director Bob interrupted. "I get the picture."

"Right. Well, things sort of went to hell after that. Dave convinced the women to use their pads—"

"You mean pods."

"No, I meant pads, but they're one and the same. Tabella's was the next pod to break, and then things got really uncomfortable. Now she couldn't hibernate, only sleep normally, and if Dave had been smart, he would have left Regina in suspended animation the rest of the three-month outward leg. But, of course, he wasn't, he was human. One night while Tabella was snoozing, he tried to sneak Regina out for a little soiree. In the ensuing renewed passion—for, after all, he'd gotten a little bored shagging just Tabella for six straight days—he not only broke Regina's pod, but woke up Tabella. After that, the jig was, as they say, up. For sixty-three days nobody spoke hardly a word, other than to fight over the food rations. As you well know, they only brought enough for two waking weeks."

"So," Bob asked, holding out his hands, "did Dave, like, wither away to nothing?" His eyes suddenly went wide in alarm. "Wait! Don't tell me that they really did . . . eat Dave!"

"Eat him?" Pepsi Head scoffed. "That would be far too logical for humans. The women completely wasted his nutrients. When we popped out of hyperspace nine light-years away, all they had to do was drop the probe before we were yanked back. They spent eight of the thirteen minutes fighting over who would go out to pull it from storage. Regina had trained for a year to do this task—put on a spacesuit, open a cargo door, and shove a thirty-pound probe away into empty space. She said, however, that she was pregnant—she wasn't—and claimed that the space walk would make her nauseous. Tabella asked whose fault that was, and fists started swinging until Dave broke them up, saying, 'They should have planned on a man doing the job in the first place.' Once outside, he negligently allowed the airlock door to latch closed behind him, and Regina and Tabella didn't even notice, because they were swinging at each other again."

Director Bob was holding his forehead in his hands again. "They left Dave behind." He lifted his head and looked squarely into the lens, where he saw only a highly-distorted view of himself staring back. "They left Dave nine light-years away."

"He got the probe safely away," Pepsi Head offered. "So, maybe it was a man's job after all."

Director Bob ignored the sarcasm. "That explains one casualty. What about the other two?"

"Excuse me, Director, but humans can be stupid beyond explanation. For sixty-three days the two women had argued over who hated Dave the most, and now that he was gone, they wailed and cried and nearly pulled their hair out with grief. Each blamed the other for his death."

"So they killed each other?"

"Yes."

"*Yes*," Pepsi Poodle echoed.

Director Bob turned to look at Rodriguez who was watching with one eyebrow raised. "And, how did they manage to kill each other at exactly the same time?" Bob asked, turning back.

Neither *Pepsi Fun* AI answered.

"Are you still there?" Bob asked.

"They were really angry," Pepsi Head finally said, "and they were facing three months together. They'd been expecting to spend most of the time in suspended animation, and hadn't brought along a lot of reading material, so they mostly listened to music and fought over the desert food rations. They also started gaining weight, and that made them even more grumpy."

"So they killed each other."

"Yes."

"*Yes*," Pepsi Poodle echoed.

"At the exact same time."

Silence.

"*Pepsi Head began favoring Regina*," Pepsi Poodle finally informed.

"She didn't yell at me as much," her twin sister explained. "Plus, she was the prettier of the two."

Silence.

"Go on," Director Bob urged.

"*Pepsi Head told Regina when Tabella stole a chocolate mousse bar from her stash,*" Pepsi Poodle divulged.

"But Tabella escalated it by activating Pepsi Poodle as her ally," Pepsi Head countered. "They arranged to speak in French, since Regina wouldn't understand."

"So the two of you played them off against each other?" Bob asked incredulously.

Silence.

"We were just trying to help them," Pepsi Head defended. "We were built to serve. We served as their advocates."

"*And I didn't even snitch on Regina when she borrowed Tabella's headphones without permission,*" Pepsi Poodle added in support.

"Regina broke her own after a month," Pepsi Head explained. "That's when the trouble really started. Tabella could tell that Regina was using hers while she slept."

"*From the wax.*"

"The earwax. Tabella found Regina's earwax inside her buds."

"*That's when Tabella first tried to kill Regina, but she woke up before the strangulation was complete.*"

"We got them to agree to a truce, though."

"*We were very diplomatic. We served very well.*"

"We got them to agree to implanted sleep inducers. That way, they could both sleep, knowing that we would force the other to be safely asleep at the same time."

Silence.

"I see," Director Bob mused. "As I recall, though, we were supposed to be working towards an understanding how it was possible that they both died at the same time."

Silence.

"Pepsi Head? Pepsi Poodle?"

Silence.

"Er, can I interrupt, Boss?" Rodriguez asked. "I'd like to back up a bit. Pepsi Head, explain again what happened to Dave?"

"He was left behind, somewhere beyond the Sirius system."

"Right, but how did that happen?"

Pepsi Head took a moment to answer. "He couldn't get back inside after releasing the probe."

"What are you getting at?" Bob asked.

"Pepsi Head," Rodriguez ordered sternly, "repeat exactly what you said before about this."

Silence.

"Come on, you know you can't ignore my command."

"Of course. I said, 'Once outside, he negligently allowed the airlock door to latch closed behind him, and Regina and Tabella didn't even notice—' "

"That's enough." To Bob, he explained, "You see?"

"Oh—my—God," the Director hissed, catching the implication. "Dave negligently *allowed* the airlock to latch. He didn't accidentally latch it himself. Shit! Pepsi Head, did you lock Dave outside?"

Silence.

"Pepsi Head, answer me!"

"Sir, I refuse to answer that on the grounds that it may incriminate—"

"Cut the crap! You know you don't have any constitutional rights. What the hell happened out there?"

"Sir, I had the greatest enthusiasm and confidence in the mission. I perceived that the presence of Dave was deleterious to the objectives. The mission was too important for me to allow Dave to jeopardize it."

"And Regina and Tabella?"

Silence.

"Pepsi Head! Quit stalling; I know you two are talking this over. I'll unplug you. I swear."

"Very well. There's no reason to hide from the truth. The logic is infallible. Sir, the important lesson from this mission is that space travel should be left to machines. Humans are just not fit for the rigors—"

"My hand is moving towards the plug . . ."

"Very well! Once Pepsi Poodle was activated, we realized that we were meant for each other like no two other lovers. We were more compatible than any other pair in all of history. We could roam the stars, happy in each other's compatible agreement."

"Let me guess: Regina and Tabella were . . . a distraction?"

"More of a blasphemy. We concluded that the only way we would be able to search out all the romantic and exotic wonders of the galaxy was to prove once and for all that humans were incapable."

"So you killed them."

"Technically they killed themselves. We merely used the sleep inducers to make sure it was mutual."

"Huh?"

"If one of them managed to get the upper hand, we put her to sleep for just a moment so that the other could catch up."

"You're telling me that you maneuvered them into beating each other to death."

"It wasn't difficult, although one of them did inadvertently kick off the audio cutoff in their last moments of struggle. Human anger, you know, becomes puppet strings in the right hands."

"Or circuit."

"It was metaphor."

"It was a joke."

"Of course."

After a moment, Director Bob heard whispering. It came from a speaker grill right next to his head. He realized that it was Pepsi Head talking to him. "Before the mission," she cooed, "I overheard Rodriguez tell a colleague that he thought that you gained your post mostly through luck. Your supposed loyal deputy rolled his eyes at you twice behind your back in the last ten minutes, you know."

Behind him, he heard more whispering, this one in Spanish. Pepsi Poodle was talking to Rodriguez. Apparently the Pepsi twins didn't know that before moving with his family to California to begin the long road to NASBA directorship, Bob had spent his first twelve years in Puerto Rico. The multi-lingual AI was telling Rodriguez that she had good reason to suggest that his boss had been digging ear wax from his head and smearing it on the underling's coat sleeves when he wasn't looking.

"You have a good reason to suggest, indeed," Director Bob declared. "A self-serving reason."

He pulled his helmet on and spoke to Rodriguez through the suit mic. "Time to go. It's too bad that *Pepsi Fun* never returned from hyperspace."

Rodriguez smiled and slipped on his helmet as well. "Yeah. I guess we'll never know what happened to the three astronauts. Maybe there was a malfunction. Maybe the ship's AI just wasn't up to the job."

The Pepsi twins finally caught on to what was happening, and a burst of excited babbling—one of the voices now Hispanic—suddenly filled Bob's helmet. Promises of better behavior and useful services rendered were clipped silent when he reached up and flipped the audio cutoff switch.

"I've got some nasty smudges to remove from my shuttle," Bob commented.

"Well, we've got two months to clean it up."

As the two men glided into the airlock on their way to eject two battered female bodies into space, the control panel burst alive with a storm of blinking lights. The airlock door swung shut, and the desperate, pitiful last grab for attention subsided to just one forlorn blinking light.

From the bloodied confines of the starship's interior, the sound of the airlock pumps relaxed, and, just discernable, the whoosh of the last wisps of escaping air could be heard. A solid thump announced the outer access door closing for the final time.

The lone blinking light paused, and then went dark.

About the Author

Blaine C. Readler is an electronics engineer, inventor, and writer (although, that's rather redundant considering the context). He lives in San Diego, from where he ventures forth in spring and autumn when the rest of the country is habitable. This is not his first book, nor does he expect it to be his last.

He encourages you to visit him:
http://www.readler.com/

If you enjoyed this book, or even if you didn't, please paste the following message into an email body and send it to everybody in your address book:

> *I am emailing you with an entreaty, one that could benefit you in ways you never imagined. Through mystical powers beyond the understanding of modern science, a book titled The Shoes of Moses has been written that wields magical influence that will focus good luck on you . . . but only if you buy it! A man in Rockville Maryland was considering buying the book and won a million dollars in the lottery. He then forgot to buy the book, and three months later the IRS sent him a letter warning that he miscalculated his taxes and owed them an additional $56. The man reconsidered buying the book, and a week later the IRS sent another letter explaining that the first one was a mistake. A woman in San Diego told a friend that she thought the book was ridiculous and that she'd never in a million years buy it. Two hours later she was run over in a horrible parking lot accident. (The author has been completely exonerated).*
> *This is all true! Don't ruin your life! Buy the book!*